The Winnebago Mysteries

Moira Crone

The
Winnebago Mysteries
and Other Stories

FICTION COLLECTIVE

Acknowledgements
"The Brooklyn Lie" and "Defining Affairs" appeared originally in
The Falcon. "Having Always Confused My Body With Hers"
appeared in *The Washington Review of the Arts.* "The Kudzu"
appeared originally in *The Ohio Review.* Portions of "The Winnebago Mysteries" have appeared in *Gallimaufry Journal* and in *Cen-
terwords: An Anthology of the Washington Women's Art Center.*
"During a Night in the Winter" appeared originally in *Gallimaufry
Journal.* "Cleanliness" appeared in *The City Paper,* Baltimore, Mary-
land, August 10, 1979.

First edition, 1984
Second printing, 1984

Published by Fiction Collective, c/o Flatiron Book Distributors, 175 Fifth Ave.
NYC 10010.

Typeset by Open Studio in Rhinebeck, N.Y., a non-profit facility for writers,
artists and independent literary publishers, supported in part by grants from
the New York State Council on the Arts and the National Endowment for the
Arts.

For the people who imagined I might do this:
Rodger Kamenetz, Mary MacArthur, and my mother

Contents

The Kudzu

By April, the camellias bloom and rot quickly in the rains. The trees are heavy with their own leaves, and the kudzu is thriving. It isn't yet summer on the calendar. I knew that in other places the trees were short. There was a boundary between spring and summer. Flowers had their seasons according to the seed packages. In other forests floors were clean, and hiking was unencumbered. Those hikes lent themselves to clear thinking about heaven.

On our walks in the woods, we had the hunters to worry about. And the water moccasins, the chiggers, red ticks and the rises in the river. But foremost in my father's mind was the kudzu and how to kill it.

He talked about the kudzu often when he was alone with me. He tried herbicides. He tried hiring men to plow it under in the autumn.

It was there before we came. It lived in a hollow carved out by the North Carolina Highway Department. They dug a hole deep as a quarry in one end of the land in the 1930's, and hauled away red clay for roads. The vines were planted for a cover crop.

We moved into the dog-trot two story house Father bought from spinster sisters called the Islers. The kudzu was just beginning to creep along the far rim of the fallow fields between the house and the hollow. Father didn't intend to set out tobacco on those tired fields. The Isler family had done that for too long.

But he was afraid the kudzu would get to the house in one summer if the fields were left unplanted.

So he rented the land to a man who planted soybeans, a hog food at the time. The man paid him hardly anything and brought orange tractors and sacks of fertilizer. Trucks full of men from the county were parked out back under the pecan tree.

That first summer the soybeans were losing to the kudzu. The fields were worn down from forty-five years of tobacco. Right as he said it, the vines were climbing over the tops of the plants, yellowing the scant crop.

Father said he could count the years on one hand before it climbed to the house, which was at least a half-mile from the hollow. I imagined it strangling the new crepe myrtles Momma bought from the nursery. In my dreams it grew on top of the Isler pear trees. It wrapped around the pecan grove and blanketed the earth beneath the trees.

When I went to girl scout camp they took us on a hike to an old brown house overgrown with kudzu vines. We walked inside to see upholstered furniture and a big Zenith T.V. The dishes were moldy in the sink. The beds were stirred and a whole family's clothes still hung in the closets. Objects were strewn: a Penny's catalogue, a patent leather pocketbook. Black dogbones lay on the braided rug by a Warm Morning heater. "Nobody knows why these people left, why they left everything," the counselor said, lifting a mildewy nightgown off the double bed.

Sundays were a certain way. My father and I went to Sunday school at St. Luke's Methodist. We drove home to get Momma to take her to eleven o'clock services, passing the Episcopal and the Presbyterian, the Baptist and the Pentecostal Holiness churches, reading the sermon marquees: "Yes, Our Brother's Keeper," "In the Valley of the Shadow," "Lying Down Beside the Troubled Waters," "Two by Two Toward the Lord." When we got to the house Momma was primping in the downstairs bathroom. She took out her bobbie pins one by one. Her hair was in a loose style from the war. The pillow-soft thickness of her hips stuck out under her half-slip. Six heavy silver bracelets jangled when she gestured. Father's black Chrysler drove into the yard and he sent me in to get her.

When I opened the bathroom door, the windows were steamy. Lilac talc dotted the floor. At the mirror, Momma sucked in her cheeks to make her mouth a dark azalea with a sable brush. She colored a beauty mark on her chin. She daubed her face with a damp sponge dipped in pancake powder and did her eyebrows with a crayon. She didn't notice me until I spoke.

She had no idea it was almost eleven o'clock since she had trouble keeping up with her watch. She said she'd be right out. I told Father.

One of his legs hung half out of the car. He read the newspaper with one elbow propped on the steering wheel. When I came back he closed the door and started the car. The radio went on again: Brother Billy Sanderson out of Charlotte. He watched the minutes by clearing his throat and honking up phlegm into his handkerchief. Momma came when she was good and ready. She told Father it is fashionable to be late.

Momma was raised an American in Cuba, and in Gulf cities like Galveston and New Orleans. She was a brought-up Catholic woman with a low forehead who didn't believe in what she called organized religion. She didn't go to bible classes, she didn't learn to drive, and she didn't go to the beauty parlor. She hated to do things other people did.

If Momma was not at all ready, she told me to tell Father she couldn't find anything to wear, or she wasn't feeling well. He got angry and told me to get in the car. We sped to the Methodists.

Later, we went back to get Momma for a ride through the county in the Chrysler. It was like a boat, with parallel chrome bars wide across its front and a crest in the middle like a capped tooth. Father pulled off the road sometimes, to curse the kudzu. He showed us how the vines had done in whole livelihoods. He pointed out examples: a rusted-down Dodge, an abandoned plow in the middle of what was once a field, all under a web of vines.

When I was six, it snowed for the first time in my life. Father bought me a sled and took me down to the hollow. I had on red rubber Woolworth's boots and white stretch socks on my hands for gloves. Momma stayed inside by the fire in her wool coat from Norfolk.

Father pushed me down the steepest incline until the snow

began to disappear in the sun. The kudzu was exposed. The sled runners slashed through the vines. Even though I was very cold, Father had me march along the whole rim of the hollow, making me sled down here and now here and now here.

The leaves looked dead and brown under the snow. But by March, the kudzu was creeping a few feet every week. It lived through the winter in its roots not its vines.

Father said that the fields couldn't grow a crop worth harvesting. And the kudzu would tear right across them if we didn't stop it.

The part of the hollow that didn't touch on fields bordered a woods of mostly sassafras and oaks that stopped at the Little River. The vines were running over the tops of those trees making a canopy that spanned towards the water. It crept up the trunks of the young pines. Normal vines like honey-suckle and wild morning glories died off in a few seasons. Places in the woods were dark in the middle of the day.

Some Sundays, Momma made us so late to church we had to wait out most of the service in the vestibule with the ushers. Father gauged from the bulletin how much we'd missed. During a pause between the offering and the sermon, the usher let us go in. We marched upstairs into the balcony which was half-filled with stragglers and teenaged girls in flat pumps and cinnamon hose. Momma always wore waisted dresses. In the summer, her floral print shirtwaists opened to her breasts, flattering her nice top and hiding her big fanny. The ladies under hats with nets on the front rows turned around to look: my mother's tanned neck showed and her bracelets made a racket. I was wearing a dress with a velveteen cummerbund. We followed behind Father, solemn in his suit.

Now and then, we missed services entirely because of Momma. She argued with Father until half-past eleven. Finally he'd stomp out of the house alone, and take me to the cemetery, which was a kind of holiday. His family's plot was trimmed every so often by a man he paid in the mail. His parents were buried under rectangles of blackish ivy. Between the graves was a thin layer of sand crystals, with gray loam underneath. Father said the water oak shading that part of the cemetery leached everything away so no grass would grow.

"But kudzu doesn't need soil to live on," he'd tell me, pointing out how it grew in the thin air along power lines. It took over dying trees and felled them. It made things into mounds with places for animals to hide.

When I took my school friends into our woods, I looked to see if the kudzu had reached the river. We went down to the hollow to play king of the mountain. Father told me to pull the vines out by their roots.

After the winter it snowed, Momma said the house was too dreary. Men came in to paint it a pastel salmon she was fond of. She had the porch railing and pillars replaced with wrought iron in a rose pattern. Plants were set out to trail up the front of the house. She had the nursery deliver coleuses and grape ivy to put inside. In the room off the kitchen where the Isler sisters were born, she put in an elephant philodendron tree that pushed through the low tongue-and-groove wood ceiling. I played in the fern boxes in the living room. Once I knocked a geranium off the porch. She cried about it on her yellow chaise lounge near the tall canna lilies. She smoked Bel-Airs and drank Pepsis there on nice afternoons.

Another man came in to lay a slate patio. Momma filled the table tops in the den with African violets lit by reading lamps. They bloomed without ever resting.

Momma didn't know why Father worried about the kudzu. She told him we weren't farmers. He could have some men come and plow poison right into the soil. Father said the poison it would take to kill the kudzu would make the fields a barrens. With the shubbery coming in you can't see them from the house, she told him.

In the hottest part of the summer Momma sunbathed behind the canna lilies on a blanket. I'd come upon her baking asleep in the sun, naked to the waist, her brown nipples pointing at the hot sky. She didn't want Father to know she sometimes sunbathed bare.

He worked very late at his office and stayed out of town seeing clients in Burgaw or Wilmington. When it was hot, he liked to walk down to the river to see if it was high. He checked the fields towards the hollow. It was hard for Momma to go hiking with us since she scratched her legs. Burrs got caught in her clothes. Wood ticks hid under her hair, at the nape of her neck.

The third summer we lived there, Father told me the kudzu would be at the edge of the garden in another season.

He was a thin man, over six feet. His hair turned gray when he was thirty. It was cut close to his head ever since the Navy. He met Momma while he was an officer. She said they used to always go to dances, during the war. There were still dresses in her closets from then—colorful and strapless. She wore them to the few parties she went to with crinolines and spiked heels.

Momma argued with Father about pruning back the fruit trees too far. She said he gave too much money to the church. She didn't like his family. Or his practice. She hated living so far from a big city. He complained of her expenses, and told her she was slovenly. She wanted to know why he ate so little so quickly and why he wasn't home enough. If she was very upset she locked the bedroom door and drank rum and Pepsi-Cola. Father swept up the kitchen so vigorously the whole bottom of the house shook. Bananas and tomatoes fell off the top of the refrigerator where Momma had them ripening. Potted plants dove off the counter, so Father would have to sweep up that, too, cursing at everything.

One Sunday Momma slept through church. When we got home, Father went out behind the canna lilies to talk to her. He startled her. They began to argue. I went around to the front of the house. In about an hour, Father came in the kitchen slamming the door. He had Momma's empty soft drink bottles. He called me on the porch.

He told me to go down to the Isler's tobacco barn and bring him some empty fertilizer sacks and tobacco stakes. He said not to disturb my mother. When I came back, he took the sacks to the well and ran the spigot on them. He told me to carry the splintery gray poles and follow him.

We walked down towards the hollow along the edge of the fields. They were planted in alfalfa and plowed under for fodder that summer. The kudzu was running along the forest, closer to the house than I remembered from a month before.

Father was wearing heavy gauge blue jeans, a loose white shirt and street shoes. I had on my blue sneakers. My hair flopped down my back in hanks. The closer we got to the hollow, the more trouble we had walking through the vines.

Father stopped at a place in the middle of the edge of the hollow, licked his thumb, and held it up. Then he pointed the direction he wanted me to walk away from him twenty paces.

Taking out his silver lighter, he set the kudzu on fire. It caught more quickly than he expected.

He went in front of the blaze, beating it back with a damp burlap sack. He told me he had it under control. Then one of his sacks was burning. The fire spread back to where I had left the tobacco sticks which were as good as kindling. He told me to keep a certain distance from the flames when I saw the burlap was drying from the heat. First he told me to help him and then he said to stay clear. He shouted at me that the fire would stop at the empty fields.

It went along the whole rim of the hollow towards the woods. His face was scorching red : he was covered with water from his eyes and his pores. He stood there encircled on three sides, telling me to keep away. I was afraid to move.

I couldn't hear him for the noise of the fire and the new low wind. Heat rippled close to the ground and the woods were beginning to burn. His face and arms were the color of a fresh bruise. Father was crying when he told me to get help.

I took off towards the house. The earth was freshly plowed. My feet sank in past my ankles. I stumbled in a furrow and saw my father behind me, half-hidden in the curling heat, waving at the fire with his arms. Then he started coming towards me. When I got to the garden, I woke Momma in the canna lilies where she said she was having a good dream. Father called the fire departments in two counties. Momma insisted she take this plant and that silver, but Father pulled her out of the house with a change of decent clothes. As he slammed the Chrysler door on her side, the pecan grove caught fire.

The Brooklyn Lie

I was sixteen and I knew what I was doing. I told my whole family a lie. After I told it, they slipped away from me while they were coming closer, as in a dream.

When I told it, I was sitting in the cabbage roses easy chair next to a mahoghany motorola. It was my grandmother's in Brooklyn, dark brick with wine carpet. She had taken up the rubber runners for the holiday. When they heard me lie, all the women in my family paced around me in circles and breathed shallowly. My father stood at the top of the stairs in stocking feet, hollow as a bottle.

After a few minutes, Grandma took a seat and a drink and a piece of Ebinger's chocolate cake. Mother went upstairs to wash her face, and later she chose not to talk to Father but to cater to me. Great-Aunty Bertha, who complained of her veins, disappeared into the Mexicali yellow kitchen. And none of it was ever the same.

To begin where I ought to, I was fat. I had been decent and simple and had long waving hair until I was fifteen. But then I was sixteen and the general misery of the world ambushed my life. I cried in biology class over pinned dragonflies, over frog's eggs triggered into tadpoles with electric shocks. I had lost my first love.

I found him during my fourteenth summer in a pavillion at Breezy Point in stretch trunks. Father spied us from a great distance making out along a strand on the beach. He smelled screwdrivers, so he said, on my new boyfriend's breath. There were screwdrivers, tequila sunrises, Budweisers and sometimes Camels there that summer. Father knew of everything and told me my boyfriend was good for nothing as well as Italian.

In the fall we used the living room couch in front of a mirror which faced the pastel drapes. When Father came in the front door, I had Jerry cover his lap with a pillow. His whole name was Jerome DeCarlo and I never did touch it. While we french-kissed, I kept my ears open for the sound of Father's car spreading gravel in the drive. I listened in case he might sneak in through the dinette.

It got so the weight of Father's steps anywhere in the house made Jerry sit up or flee. If Father cleared his throat in the upstairs bedroom, Jerry was out on the stoop and full of so-longs.

When Jerry's father drove us to a dance or the movies and brought us home ten minutes late, Father met us at the door, and scared Jerry off the porch. Then he hit me with his shoes. He chased me around the upstairs as I undressed.

I threatened Father with marrying Jerry just to get out of the house. Once when Jerry stayed for dinner I broke the ice with, "When Jerry and I get married, I'll cook..." at which Father choked on his spiced apple and almost coughed into the next world. My older sister circled his chest with her arms, something she learned in nursing school. He went from blue to red.

Later, my sister tried to explain to me: Father is having climacteric so is Mother. I was the younger and more precocious. She wondered that I didn't have an evil streak. And Father wasn't always pleased with how the years had turned out. Father was sensitive. He was a druggist. I was callow and a nothing. I did not know about marrying or happiness even. My whole world was this dark silly boy. My world was stubby and tiny. I did not know about life. So I banged my fists on my skull and ran downstairs out of sorrow.

Jerry came by everyday. He brought me gifts he had stolen: cash from the typing teacher's drawer, an XKE hubcap, a pink water pistol. He called me every night. Father protested the length of the calls which were cheap and local. Jerry lived sixteen blocks away on Nostrand. And it was not the family phone, but mine, a Princess Father got for me when I was unpopular. When Jerry called, I closed the double doors to my room, lay on my tummy on the stained wood floor and drew with a ballpoint on the skirt of the vanity while Father banged and knocked. He never hit Jerry in person. But Jerry figured it was an oversight my father would sooner or later correct.

Then, as it is with fate, Jerry's family went to Montclair for the weekend. He didn't call the night he got back. He called the next day. He came over, but he seemed reluctant. Father was in watching golf. It was a Sunday in mid-summer. We had been together two whole years. I was wearing Bermudas and Jerry mentioned I was gaining weight.

Then he said he had made it with his cousin in a Jersey swim club shower. She was a girl-lifeguard. He said I could never keep my mind on it so there must be something wrong with me. I told him I was brought up Irish Catholic. I needed warming up. Jerry said any girl at St. Vincent's would go down, so answer me.

We broke up.

I tried getting him back with sympathetic magic.

I used incense, mink oil and chanting, Lourdes Water, and phone calls to his mother. I tried to follow the advice in magazines. I got him to come over and play records and eat candy. I told him I would do it, but the thrill was dead. He said I was getting sloppy fat.

For months after Jerry left, I cried at four o'clock in the afternoon to satisfy a habit. My school was all girls in plaids. There were no other boys. My hair started falling out. My cycles stopped. Mother took me to a doctor who asked why I was so sad. "Why do you sigh instead of breathe? Is there something in your throat?" I told him pieces of my broken heart. He gave me pills to lift my spirits, hormones which made me perpetually hungry. My breasts became purple from the stretching. My sister gasped when she saw me undress.

Father and Mother went about their business. They gave me compliments, which are cheap. I ate ice cream and went to bed as much as possible.

Then, in November, 1963, we went across Brooklyn for Thanksgiving at my Grandma's. I had already made up my mind to leave the family and live my own life. If I ran away I could be one of them, the girls I saw in Washington Park when I sneaked there on Sundays. They wore their hair loose to their elbows.

Right before I told the lie, I was sitting at the kitchen table opposite Momma and my sister the nurse named June. At twenty she looked exactly like my mother. We were talking and picking at the food. Grandma was tall and bony, her pencil legs in support hose. She and little Aunty Bertha who was quite fat and wore a two-piece navy suit, were doing dishes, shining things, and putting them up.

"I am running away," I said.

"Where would you go? Red Hook?" Grandma asked. I didn't know if there was a Red Hook anymore. To Grandma it was the Brooklyn word for hell. She also believed I'd be sold into white slave trade if I went to Greenwich Village. "Where, off to the Village where they will slip you a Mickey Finn—and you wake up in the bottom of a ship at sea?"

Mother began, "You wouldn't have to slip her anything. She has worse in mind than that."

"I do not take drugs."

"Yes you do." It was my sister. She was lying.

"Look who is talking. The Benzedrine queen. How'd you get through your exams, sis?"

"What do you have to get away from home for, then?"

"You and Poppa. You make me sick."

Grandma gasped.

"That might be reciprocal." Mother answered.

"Send me to a cheap prep school. Somewhere they'll pay to have me. I can get some kind of scholarship."

"To reform school." Mother picked up an icy new Vermouth.

"I make good grades."

"Eighty-eight last report card in geometry. Mooning all the time over that Italian hood."

My sister added, "Send her away, Momma. She needs some discipline in her life. She's wasting away in Brooklyn."

"I'm not sending her anywhere. Not even to a psychiatrist."

"I hate you." I was telling the truth. "I hate your fat back and your fingers and your smelly husband—"

Grandma and Aunty Bertha were perfectly still, their tie-up black shoes sticking to the floor. Mother was about to slap me. My sister stepped forward, "She's a baby and she doesn't know what she's saying. Let her go. Don't hold onto your baby, Momma." She turned to me, holding her mouth in a sophisticated way I wouldn't trust. "Look. Mother is suffering from Empty-Nest. Go easy."

"What do you know Nightingale? You aren't stuck with them. You got away already." My sister boarded at nursing school. "Tweet-tweet."

"Stop this in my house. Out with all of you." Grandma was overruled. The other women at the table were meaner and fatter, stronger and louder than she. My sister turned again to Mother. "Send her anywhere. She only makes you miserable."

Mother was pulling at her unretouched roots. I told her she was fat, ugly, awful and menopausal. Finally she came back —

"YOU NEVER LET UP DO YOU?"

That was it. I never saw her like this before. She was crazy. I yelled she should be committed. Then we were going through the swinging doors to the dining room, Mother shoving me with her pounding fists. "You're losing control," I told her. My sister was trying to get in between us. When Mother lunged, I went head down through the archway into the easy chair in the livingroom.

My sister and my mother were holding each other now, as if the world were coming to an end, which was true.

Then Father's flat stocking foot appeared near the top of the stairs. His thick leg in gray trousers came next, then his bright amber velour sweater someone gave him by mistake, thinking his eyes were brown.

"WHAT THE HELL IS GOING ON?"

For these few seconds I had the dead middle of everyone's thoughts. The silence was sharp and very visible. Mother loosened herself from my sister's arms and told Father I was a monster.

Grandma stood with a handful of good silver, the fork tongs pointing in every direction. All my work and my whole life, she was thinking, and still the family is unhappy.

Mother looked up at Father, Father looked down towards me

and Grandma and my sister pointed at my plain closed face. The miserableness in everyone was beyond knowing and without reason, it seemed. I didn't want to cry. I felt a certain lightness. This was a kind of joke, over the pudgy girl in the chair, something the family made up, an amusement.

"I'm pregnant," I said.

It seemed to follow.

The grown women in the room first wandered and then settled. Bertha came out of hiding in the kitchen holding a drink for her sister. She slipped away again, to sob. My father put his head into his hands, sat down on the step, and looked into the wine carpet. My sister took Mother upstairs to wash her face.

They did not ask me how I knew. They forgot that Jerry and I were long caput. It may have been my strange ballooning breasts, but everyone believed. They had faith and suddenly they sat quietly. Our youngest is having a child. They did not ask whose, and they asked nothing else. My sister was not even curious.

Just Aunty Bertha, who was maiden and very small. She came to my bedside late that evening to ask, "How could you be so dirty?" The rest of the night the people in my family, usually so unsure of themselves, came towards me deliberately to kiss me or feed me. I was no longer their own. Everyone told me they loved me.

In the morning, Father took me for a ride in his Impala. He drove me through every borough, Queens, Manhattan, the Bronx, pointing at buildings and telling me what they used to be. He told me what was wrong with his life, with his marriage, with my mother. These were things I never heard from him before. The family was over. He also said he thought I was pretty. He was a grown man I was riding with in a car. And I was no longer a daughter but I was bloated, soft, crazy and delighted.

During a Night in the Winter

They pass out on the bed after a spaghetti supper. Lena tells him they catch sleepiness from one another. And that the lovemaking is wearing them down.

First he has a dream of her smile, which makes him uneasy. Then of his mother, the tiny empty face beside his father. She is the carrier of the balding genes that are inactive in women. Their heads are really large hairballs, as much inside them as out like trees with the same mass of roots as branches: Some women have ovarian cysts made out of hair or human teeth. Some female animals generate spontaneously from electric shock: a small, split suede genital dangling and purplish, the thighs moving, under everything, a steaming laugh.

He gets up and goes to the bathroom. Then he puts on a reggae record. She looks out the window: the sky is beige. It is eight. She closes her eyes again. She sees Gene with some woman in a light gray boring dream. It is herself, she perceives. They are iceskating. They fall through a crack and the water beneath is gelatin. She is too tired to watch the ending. She sits up for good.

In the hot bed, all the blood in her body is pumping under her navel. Some of it dribbles onto her legs, and bits of glitter spread around her brain, which is dark from lying down.

"You've watered your avocado to death," he tells her.

"I know. I'm planning on re-potting it tomorrow night. No drainage in that pot." She puts her feet on the green nylon carpet. "Do you remember that film, with the guy who starred in *If*? It had something to do with a salesman? Remember?"

"What about it?"

"You know, he's English, with a big nose."

"Get dressed."

"I am dressed."

He comes over to her and kisses her stomach. She opens the zipper of her pants, and lets him reach in.

"Come on. We are supposed to go over to Jerome's."

"Don't I look pretty?"

He squeezes her breasts as if testing for something. "Yea." They begin to dance, Lena pulling him up.

"Turn off the music now." He is a clumsy dancer.

"Gene?"

"Huh?"

"I love your coloring, you know that? You are brighter than anything in the snow."

He's uncomfortable with the remark, it makes him helpless. He feels like a kid trying to learn to dress, something he knows is supposed to be very easy. His brothers did it. He goes toward the door. As she grabs her coat he goes down the stairs out of the house. She wonders if she left a cigarette burning. She opens the door again. Pops some ju-jubes from a cellophane bag in the kitchen into her mouth. One black, one green, one yellow, shaped like papooses. She turns off the bathroom light. He is yelling at her from the bottom of the stairs.

In the car she asks him, "Do you remember the scene, where that actor, the one with the big nose, is running up and down the hall, in some kind of experimental hospital, and he finds his friend wheezing and crying, covered with a sheet in a little room? He lifts up the sheet and the friend's head has been grafted onto a hog's body. Did you see that movie?"

"No."

"There is another part where he goes to heaven."

Gene's car is stuck in first gear, sounding as if it is breaking its heart.

"Momma told me today on the phone that small cars are very cheap right now. She didn't call me for any reason. Does your mother call you all the time?" She lights a cigarette while he tries to adjust his gearshift. "I don't like Jerome. And I can never seem to have a conversation with his girlfriend. What's her name?"

"I've told you fifty times, she's Jill. She's a fine woman. She's easy to talk to. You must have a block or something."

They pull up to the apartment house. Inside, Jill is fiddling with a jack-loom in the living room. Then she goes into the kitchen. Gene, Lena, and Jerome start to argue around the dining room table. Jill interrupts them to say it has started snowing as she tucks the label back into her turtleneck. Lena follows her into the kitchen, trying to think of something to say to her. Lena wants to say she feels sick from sleeping so much. Or to ask her why she never talks but lumbers around instead, as if she were rearranging the apartment whenever they come over. As if some other guests were expected. Finally she asks for some aspirin and water. While she rinses the dishes, Jill says she just found out she is pregnant. Lena says, "Beautiful." In a lot outside the window, the snow falls like flour filling a bowl.

"Look, I make more aesthetic choices tuning the T.V. than Albert. Give me a break." Reaching for coffee, Jerome goes on in the dining room. "Tell you what. Your taste bites. But I've got something even you can get off on." He opens the door to the bedroom.

There is a small display case on the dresser. Inside are four rows of small plastic rectangles on a piece of black velveteen. Each rectangle has a small sculptured head: birds, horses, cowboys. Above the dresser is a picture of Napoleon.

"Isn't this great? What? PEZ GUNS, you idiot. I put out big bucks for this. Early Plastic." He opens the case, removes a blue gun, and flicks the top up and down. "Donald Duck. 1939. Amazing, huh?"

Later Gene tries to exit by going down the driveway on a cookie sheet. Jerome tells Lena, "Look, it's a kid's trick. Gene's too fat." Gene is stuck. "And tell your friend there, when he's sane again, that he's a—"

Lena rolls down the hill like a cylinder. Then she runs into the snow more than a block, until she can't make out Gene's car any longer. She would like to dive into a drift, but the snow is scant and wet. Her shoes pick it up.

"Gene, Jerome told me to tell you that Pearlstein is drab," she says, opening the car door. "And Jill's having a kid."

"Does Jerome know?"

"She didn't say any more. I suppose she's ideal, huh? A nice body, nothing ever to say, not even about being pregnant. She's just what men want, isn't she? I suppose we could have chatted about cooking or menstruation but I couldn't seem to get her started."

"Why are you such a bitch?" Then he starts talking about something she doesn't feel like following. They get back to her apartment. Gene goes after her into her bedroom.

She tells him to go on home. "You won't be able to drive much longer. It's bad out." She turns on the bathwater. She is looking in the mirror, at the two moles on her chin. She has an impulse to scream. Some Sardo Bath Oil into the tub, and she steps in.

"Why do you want me to go home, honey?"

"You really want to know? This is boring. I hate it sometimes, don't you?"

"Then I won't come around for a while."

"What I get out of this I get vicariously. You thank me. But I'm sick and tired of hearing about you." She rubs her arm with a loofah sponge. Drowns him out by running the bathwater. He comes into the bathroom. "Get out! I'll talk to you in a minute."

She comes out wrapped in a polka-dot towel, and sits down on the bed drawing up her legs. Snow is coming down in the triangle made by her knee, lit by the living room of the wooden house next door. The curving street goes around a hill. The town is built in tiers, out of three-story houses with stairways and cellars. Their underwear, his socks, are lost in the alley way between the bed and the wall. The Vaseline, t-shirts, a copy of the *Naomi* poems, her abalone necklace, the spilling of the ashtray on the window sill.

"I haven't occurred to you, have I?"

"What do you want? You think you know me so well?" He is close enough to her that she hears him breathe. Once, sleeping with him, she dreamed she was walking in his breath. It was noisy as a wind.

"I feel like I'm a mammal. I could be anybody. I am always making us up as we go along."

"That is supposed to be my fault? You are crazy. You and me for sitting here are crazy." She is exactly crazy. Plants can't live around her but they grow from her fingers, from her pelvis. This little room is a compartment on a train. She is a passenger who lifts up her skirt. Her lower body is turning into the woods. "But you are so open all the time. Like tonight. You think Jerome wants to hear about your last lover?"

"That's exactly what I mean."

"What?"

"Hello Jerome or anybody, Lena. What did you think of the Zweig retrospective?"

"You trying to say I'm stifling you? Oh, the little flower, Christsake. Talk."

"Okay. What would you like to know? My name is Lena. I'm twenty-two. I am okay in the sack. When I have sex I have it with Gene and a diaphragm. I eat a lot of dairy products. I get up to go to work at eight. I have six sick days left. On sick days I take huge baths and fantasize being really sick. I would like to be sick so I could start all over. From the top. My name is Lena—"

"Okay, okay. All of a sudden you want something else? You changing all the rules?" He wants her dead. He can't remember how he got into this. When he wasn't with her he didn't miss her. Now and then he wants to sleep with her. He thinks of stuffing her mouth with the polka dot towel, of how stupid she looks.

She wants to throw him through the window into the snow. She sees herself slamming the door to her apartment on him, throwing him backwards down the stairs, out the downstairs door, off the concrete stoop, onto the ice on the path, on and on until he wears away. She will kick up the seat of his chair so his back hits the radiator. She rolls over toward the window.

"Why are you so upset? You brought all of this up. You want me to leave? Do you want to quit? Okay. You are crazy, you know that?" He starts to lace up his shoes. "I never saw you like this." She has her fist in her mouth. Her other hand is on the window pane.

"I don't know what to do either. Go away. I hate us, I hate you."

He gets up. "I'm going right now."

She is pushing the door in his face. The door is in the center of the house. The stairs are down the middle. He will fall exactly backwards. He will crash through the half-glass front door.

They are both quiet. For a long time they listen to his nose whistle breath. "Leave," she says finally.

"I don't feel like telling you I love you," he tells her, sitting down again. "Why are you pulling this? What difference does it make?"

"You are making love to me." She pulls him on top of her. She is tugging at him, kissing his nose and his beard.

"Stop. We didn't finish."

"Shut up." She takes off her bathtowel. She presents, like a woman ape, she says to herself. It is me, he wants to say to her. it's my shirt, my penis. She tugs at him like something in the water. She starts breathing more slowly.

When they begin, she is thinking she is supposed to be thinking about the pleasure. A street off of William Street in the town where she grew up. Wandering there is a greenish light. An animal, a horse made out of car parts for advertising a carburetor place gallops on a concrete platform, rocking, facing the main highway, no sidewalks, nowhere to walk and she wants a place to walk. The oaks. Something about a room. A room with mauve furniture, a person sitting on the floor. People going into the next room. This is because the memory is in the heels and the neck and knees. Wherever he touches something springs up, something from the day before or the year before. She can't concentrate. They are rolling over and over each other. It isn't easy to keep on the bed. That keeps her half-awake.

Defining Affairs

In this story, about my departure from the course of fidelity to both my husband and the idiom, and my pursuant mental collapse, I will use the following new words correctly: panache, epiphany, hermaphrodite, egregious. Note that I use them deftly, i.e., with deft.

Once upon a time I was trying to finish my Ph.D. thesis on the poetry of V. Sackville-West when Mark my husband got the dictionary editorship. There are quite a few little towns within commuting distance of the Narrian-Wobbles offices. We chose Randomton because it had a college and June, a very old friend of mine. I hadn't seen her since I left the country five years before. She lived there with her husband George, a professor.

Those five years, Mark and I were in grad school at the University of South Wales. His field is the Mabinogion. When we got back to the States, the dictionary job was to pay off all our student loans, eight years altogether. And not much job market for people in our fields. He didn't do much at the dictionary, really, except listen to Public Radio to find out how new terms are pronounced. Sometimes he listened to two shows at once, scribbling all the while. He did it when he came home at night too. If I slurred "that" into a very dental "dat", he would write it down on a 3 x 5, as a variant. Same with T.V., and when we went to plays. For a while it was unnerving to me. I grew very quiet around him.

We set up in a darling little house with a front and back

porch, hardly three blocks from June's. Soon after we arrived, she had us over to dinner. Light salad, just the right amount of vinaigrette. Melon and some new friends of hers.

June's husband was very popular at the college. His field was heretical practices of the Middle Ages, in particular the debaucherous cults. The students loved it. I suggested to Mark he ought to write a course proposal entitled "Humor, Eros, and Sexuality in the Mabinogion," to break into teaching, but he refused. He said he thought that must be the Middle New England dialect creeping in, that dropped "r" in "Humor."

Meanwhile, in this little town, I was depressed. So quiet in the house all day long, you know, not even a cat. I kept expecting an epiphany to hit. Mark wanted to have a baby and name it Llwyd, or something even more Welsh, but I'm afraid we would have argued too much at the time over how to pronounce it. I had practically forgotten the language. I had spent my last six months in the country in St. Marbles Asylum, and fled the British Isles right after I was released. They spoke only English in the hospital, and I could hardly speak at all. That lapse was something Mark had never understood, even years later. I had always thought and punctuated so clearly.

I tried to see June as often as I could, but she always had to go to Tai Chi or something with her women friends. Our relationship deteriorated into her leaving me parcels of poorly written feminist literature on the porch, demanding I digest it. She begged me to go to consciousness meetings, so I could, as she said, vulnerabilize myself. This was during the nasty spring they have in New England—filthy snow that will not disappear. Greyish blots that seem to smoke when it rains freezing rain in March. Actually, it wasn't smoke but a sort of visible frigid evaporation: cold steaming from the ugly mounds. All the women at the meetings wore those puffy bright jackets, and shoes with the tire-tread bottoms.

June had her family to think of, too, along with her activism. She had her children, Jodi and Jack. Jack was a little Negro boy they adopted during the late sixties. I was out of the country for all of that.

Jodi, June's natural child, was very curious. She had a deep voice like her father's but then George has a rather weak voice for a male. And her hair was the length all professors' children were wearing their hair: Prince Valiant length. The curious thing was the child's gender. You couldn't tell right away. I say "she" since Jodi was raised a girl. But as June had remarked, Jodi's puberty had been full of surprises. I mean Jodi was growing a you-know-what, all of a sudden. I use this un-tragic, nonchalant tone since June always used it: Nothing so dreadful about having brought an hermaphrodite into the world; more everyday than you might think. Jodi was a cute tomboy with no apparent problems. Aubrey Beardsley, after all. Mark preferred the word androgyne, but I could never remember whether it had a hard "g" or a soft "g", probably from having been raised never to say gynecologist out loud.

I was quite willing to come over any time, and put up with her nasty kitchen, noise, and disarray, just to get to see her. There was usually some strange woman in the house, though, one in a large plaid shirt and blue jeans. But once I came by and June was alone, a-bloom with hives.

"Don't you realize you are covered with red blobs, June?"

"They'll go away tomorrow if Samantha comes back to me."

"June, I don't understand. Last time I saw you it was Lydia."

"Samantha has a new friend in the dorms. I saw her at Shiatsu Massage class with that globby little religion major. You know the one I mean."

"Sesamee Hams?"

"I don't think she was *born* with that name."

"Now June, why can't she have other friends? You have me, after all."

"But we were just girls then."

June had such a one-track mind. The children came by, asking for organic snacks. She gave them pumpkin seeds. What a sight she was, really, in a bright red turtleneck of all things, with four vermilion splotches on her face, ugly as birthmarks. Startling as a fire-engine.

"It's not only that," she went on. "George thinks I spend too much time with my women friends. He doesn't like me going down to the Wimmin's Bar all the time."

"You go every night?"

"Yes."

"When do you see George?"

"Sometimes we sleep in the same bed."

"But June, whenever I run into you in town, you're holding hands with another girlfriend. The laundromat, restaurants, the Vietnamese Refugee Dinners, dance concerts."

"You don't see. You don't see. It's an exploding situation. Like a super-nova. Do you understand now?"

"June, this is a very personal question. Are you a—"

I couldn't finish. The way that sort of (now I realize) unnatural affection can spread in some people. I thought of Vita and her Violet; this was before that trivial book came out. Of course. I had never understood what that meant before. June was a very happily married woman, just like me. She had George, and he had all those developed interests. I have to admit I was rather stunned.

George was coming home less and less for dinner. One night he tried, without much success, to kick a woman out of the house. June didn't seem to care whether he came home or not. I called her one evening in early summer. She came panting to the phone.

Some female laughter could be heard in the background. June giggled for five minutes.

"It's about the food co-op. How many pounds of haddock are you willing to order? We don't get it wholesale unless we get a certain amount of orders, you know. Butter? New potatoes?" (I have to admit I was very angry. She wasn't being even civil. Now there was cooing in the background.) "I'm terribly involved with someone right now," she said. Laughter increased. "I mean—"

I was livid. My joining the co-op was June's idea in the first place. I would have been perfectly happy with the Purity or the Stop and Shop. With her (and George sort of went along) it was rather a matter of conscience whom you brought your potatoes from.

In fact, I was so angry I couldn't sleep at night, thinking what I would say to June when I saw her again. She wouldn't even give me the time of day, and I had moved to Randomton entirely because of her.

Well, something snapped. When I got up in the morning, I called Mark "Muck." That was the beginning. My logic ran something like this: We are all too dependent on the prevailing definitions. It was high time we took liberties. June was certainly taking enough. Why couldn't I say panache, for example, when I didn't mean plume or anything like it? Why couldn't I say June had a certain panache for certain women? or vice-versa? See, the words get uncontainable, and I couldn't contain them. June was egregious after so-and-so. She was doggerel for LuLu, or whomever. Etc. I got so I never knew what I was going to say next.

I went and asked June if she wasn't puddy-fumbling around. Wasn't there something George should be told, and etcetera, ad infinitum blah, blah. I had never been so blunt in my whole life.

June was taken aback, and she asked me, point blank, what was I insinuating, and if it was what she thought, well then I should go ahead and be direct. I went ahead.

"That you have a, uh, flotsam for certain women." I thought that this might collapse the nice between us, if we could be scathing and utter, you know.

June agreed that my dialysis was accurate. But, she told me with rumble, all of that was last tense. Her newest love had run off with a true triangle, he an andrologist, she a rich, rich harness. June and George and sweet Jodi and black Jack were like Manhattan after the flood. "There is a whole to our vice-versa now." June rattled painfully. I told her she still had me. She took me upstairs.

We then commenced an interlope of the first magnitude. For some time, we were perfervid, clandestinely. Mark was getting suspicious, so finally I decided to tell him. I began:

"June and I've adopted the suffolk mold."

"I'm too reasonable and so forth for this." Mark remarked. "What do you mean? Is there bedding together?"

"Mares whore um you stink."

"What do you mean?"

"Whales ailing to smoke." He found it unsettling, and finally the cadaver ceased for some time, that is, we rent our separate whacks, Mark and me. Before he moved out so June could move in, I burned all his index cards, and shredded his notes in the blender. I was encroaching another lapse disaster.

June came to stay. At home we were quiet, we kept the sound turned down on the T.V. She delighted in my malapropisms. When she combed my hair, she'd bend over me and whisper:

"Muck don abidom lux. Aba dadi shoem should?"

"Stomp cheddar tub." I'd answer.

"Wonder lubiam lux lux."

"La da dee pum dawdle."

"Waxy?" She would ask, placing her sweet able mouth on my cheek.

"Dun butter dum," she'd finish, and I'd putter off to bathe, leaving her staring at the aquarium.

But April is as cruel as we've heard. Understand June and I were quite flamboyant. We carried ourselves through the streets of Randomtom with aplomb, panache, and dash. Muck my has been made big waves. He started suing June for alienation of affection. And she fled under the palaver. George was talking divorce. One morning while I was in the kitchen baking banana nut bread, some fellows in white came to the door.

"Wad obit awry?" I asked them.

"We want you to come to the state hospital. For observation," one of them told me.

"Sockbulls!" I shrieked. "Sadam! Stump!"

They wrapped me up in one of those vests with buckles so I couldn't use my arms. The next thing I knew I was sitting up in bed and Mark was reading to me.

"Abidom lux—present past participle of the verb to loathe, in Ancient Basque. Stump—chopped down tree. Thespian—actor. Suffolk mold—a growth on certain meat byproducts. Repeat after me, dear..."

And that's how I snapped back. But I've never been quite the same since. I lost my high I.Q. this time. I don't understand Sackville-West anymore. And I still have this problem of not knowing what I mean. But Mark has been very good about telling me.

The lapses are more and more infrequent, since treatment. Oh, I didn't mention the treatment. See first paragraph. I hope awfully I've been accurate. I've got back the ability to do library work, and built up to a point that I can use reason with Mark as well as pronunciation, diction and meaning. When I'm done with this, Mark will correct it. Rather like rehabilitation after a stroke.

When June and George finally filed for divorce, George tattled on us in court. He won a decision that she was an unfit mother since she'd left Jodi be. He got custody, and had the child treated. The last I heard, she is a boy.

*Having Always Confused
My Body with Hers*

I am with her in a foil papered booth in a Cambridge restaurant. We've both ordered coffee with whipped cream. She tells me she is leaving her husband. Her one calf bounces wildly while the other knee keeps a sideways syncopation under the table. She is an art historian. She says she thinks she has some cigarettes.

Several blocks away her child is sleeping in her father's arms on a couch in a room where butts, books, spilled glasses, pamphlets, underwear, toys, baby clothes, stains, broken jewelry and plastic debris cover all surfaces. She is not a housekeeper. She is, however, careful to take baths, to smell sweet, and to wear clothes that may not fasten but are clean. She dwells in public places: museums, coffee counters, streets with many store windows, libraries.

"I deserve pleasure. He bores me. We should have had a friendship, never a marriage. But when I met him, who could have known? He was a manic. I'm no clairvoyant."

Before I knew of my own life, I was aware of hers. Too extreme to be a mother, she was an idol. I lived because she loved me. We had our private games. In one of them, I was to eat every bite she ate at the same moment. There were two 15 cent hamburgers on two plates, two small bags of french fries. We started at the word go. We distributed the fries so that our piles were exactly equal. Next, we took each one and brought them simultaneously to our mouths. I confused my body with hers.

Now I bring her hand to my face, observing the condition of her fingernails. When I was a child, I used to bite hers when I was done with my own. We are intimate still: our sex, spells, vanity—these are shared as other people share a pair of scissors. She is frank. We have the same phrasing, the same humor. She is one of two people in the world who upset me physically when they cry. I have to prostrate myself, take her into my arms, to teach her to believe in me again. She must know it will never change.

I watched her beige shadow in the shower stall. She was beginning breasts. The steam on the bathroom mirror cleared. I was a small dark head whose chin rested on the sink. She was a huge nacreous statue looking at herself.

It is one of the conditions of our relation that she always be the stronger. I wait for her direction. And I pay with tears when I don't love her, when I disappoint her.

She is talking about the fate of the 2,000 copies of her Ph.D. thesis that were published in Europe. A new interpretation of the Bayeaux Tapestries. I have seen them. I know what color they are. She is explaining them again. I have never learned adequately an iota of what she meant to teach me.

She meant to teach me Latin, to read, to type, to dance, to conjugate in every Indo-European language. I had to know world geography and elementary geometry. I studied Saturdays, Sundays, and the school day afternoons. She had me parsing sentences at three and a half.

But my nature was lazy, nay-saying, deliberately negligent. She never forgave me for forgetting my declensions. Or for confusing Mongolia and Montgomery. I failed at least once a month. It was always a failure of devotion. I hit my head against walls, ran and hid in the closet. But the cells in my brain, which I believed at the time could be observed by closing the eyes quite tightly, danced and scattered when I pressed my fists in my sockets or when I gripped the texts she found for me. We both have thick Germanic hands, huge for women.

She's off to a new professorship in Canada.

"Oh, I admit it," she begins. "When I get there and have to put the baby in daycare full-time, I know I'll have maybe an intense depression. But I've come out of them before. If he were to kill himself over all of this—I don't know. I'm not so nice as I once was. I used to be nice. I used to think love was the motivation behind things. Now I want to have some fun. He hasn't the get-up-and-go. And he's a young man. Frankly, I don't think he's got the guilt to kill himself. It takes a special kind, you know. What I get for marrying a genius."

I will not have another coffee at her urging. She drank half of mine and now she's having another.

She grew up: slept, fidgeted, and ate away her adolescence. She took on Elke Sommer's pout. And the gestures from the photographed soap operas in Italian magazines. She changed her name. She told me to cry with her. CRY WITH ME. I had to. We caught it from one another. There was the whole world to cry about.

"You know what I want now? A life's work. Something absolutely comprehensive. That re-interprets a whole period. Something that overturns the field. Caravaggio, maybe. Or the Pre-Raphaelites." She looks away. She has hemorrhoids again, she tells me. "I get sick of men," she adds. "You know these academic types. No imagination. Queers, anal." Her face is bright as a snowbank. It has something to do with what she is thinking, not what she is saying.

"Well, what are you up to? Don't tell this to anyone but he—no. You always spill the beans."

"I do not." I do betray her.

"You blab. I know."

"What is it?"

"Promise, don't tell anyone." She leans forward. Takes a breadstick from the basket.

"What is it?" I ask. She's not going to tell me.

"No. You blab. Momma told me something you told her you weren't supposed to tell anyone."

I know what she means. She has won. Now she is picking at her head. Her fingernail discards a fresh little hard scab on the edge of the ashtray. She pilfers the last teaspoonful of my whipped cream.

"So what are you up to?"

Depressed, I tell her.

"It's time you saw a psychiatrist. You know, the psyche can sort of be fixed once you name it. I believe that."

I don't think a shrink would do me any good.

"Don't you want to be taken seriously? That's what they are paid to do you know, to take you seriously."

I don't know.

"There is nothing else, ultimately," she tells me, "other than to be taken seriously. Everything else is dull. I know you have this spiritual dimension, but it won't keep you interesting."

We sat through THE BRIDGE OVER THE RIVER KWAI twice because it was "serious and moving." The 1950's. The same game. I had to eat what she ate because I loved her. Through both runs of the movie: red hots, popcorn, jujubes, cokes and grape drinks. The back of my legs felt stiff and the blast of heat after the refrigeration of the theatre nauseated me. The waitress came. She ordered a hot dog, and a strawberry milkshake. My turn.

"A Dr. Pepper, please. And a grilled cheese sandwich." I was scared of myself. The devil got into me. The waitress was gone before I could fix it.

"Well," I tell her. "I suppose you find my life as dull as I find yours." I can feel a little pain in the glands under my arms. "Are you ready to go?"

"I know you do, but what's duller is doing nothing about it. About the way you are given to feel about yourself. Why are we so unhappy? You are. I can tell. It runs in the family. We feel terrible. It's somebody's fault, I suppose. Who can be satisfied in this life? *Are you satisfied?* It's awful, generally, isn't it?"

I have never told her how hateful she is. That her child is already crazy.

When we are walking to my bus stop I love her again. Since her pregnancy, she's lost her center of gravity. She goes next to me in her platforms, her neck rhythmically, awkwardly stretching forward. I want to touch her arms which have a strange, extremely soft consistency. When I am near her it is the inside of her body that I know. And its surface—the silverish stretch marks across her back. The kinds of nightmares she wakes with in her twin next to mine. Her hair is always bleached and matted as ivy. I am her paper pale face, and the food in her stomach. If I walk inside her the clothes are uncomfortable: crinolines crisp as vinyl, the shoe heels too high, the lipstick bad tasting. I feel her little shooting pains, the electricity scattering in our limbs when we lie down to sleep in our childhood.

Cleanliness

Children are always less than their parents, worth, at most, ninety or ninety-five percent. Mothers keep a portion of every soul that inhabits them: This is why women with many, many children are saints. Those who bear quintuplets are canonized instantly. The world perceives their grace from simple photographs in the news wire service; they appear terribly happy; they are showered with gifts and they are sterilized.

Besides what they keep, mothers also pass things on: little marks. Their old dreams remain in their children like an indelible graffiti. Babies receive, in short, whatever their mothers would like to be rid of. And we know a woman may find her demon full blown across the kitchen in a high chair, glowering over, pressing oatmeal into its bib with an intensity unbecoming a child of light.

I am a daughter with a soul like a fist in a box. Unmarried, I bought a house with my lover which my mother Dolores went out of her way to visit. All stages of existence dwell in a house. Infancy is in the closet beside the bedroom; adolescence is in the disorganized kitchen; the middle glow of childhood is near the two rosebushes along the path to the garage. Ego is in the study and adulthood and death are in the bedroom. Whatever is at the bottom of life dwells in the cellar.

The fashion now in interiors is extremely empty rooms. It is the modern desire for flushed minds, for amnesia. I could not make my house clean enough for my mother. She would desire the rooms be at least as empty as she hoped her womb might have been, after bearing her worst and last daughter. She held back five percent, unwillingly, because the universe is stingy.

After three children, Mother grew blurrier and blurrier. She almost faded into her babies, and then into the walls of her house; becoming less and less aware of who she might have been.

The souls amidst us are hungry, it is said. After the last war, the millions who were robbed of their lives demanded indignantly to be born. I was among them. Any manifestation would do, any country, any woman. Dolores followed my father, a soldier, during her period of fertility. Their lives were swept away. In this setting, she bore babies only because she did not have any choice. And she is a perfectionist. All of her daughters are inaccurate. So are our lives: one is a brilliant scholar who is also beautiful enough to be a model, but she is poor. Another is an executive whose pregnancy is ruining her career. The last, an odd brunette, has made prodigality a way of life. This one is me, a know-nothing. We three sisters love each other nervously. Our medium of exchange is our disapproving Momma. The worst insult we know for one another is the comment, "You are reminding me of Dolores."

I tried to clean when Momma came. She told me on the phone from a distance to bleach the floors, shine the woodwork, slipcover the furniture and trim the garden. Mother could imagine this modest house. She knows small houses in cities. She was raised in one in Brooklyn with a blue door and casement windows in a four-poster maple bed that I also slept in as a child while my widowed grandmother snored and Dolores moaned in the master bedroom with her husband.

When I was born, Mother happily handed me over. She had recently moved into a bungalow in the Central South with her husband who worked very hard. She painted the bungalow the color of face powder. She had decided there was no spirit in the world, only material. She put mirrors in every room and gazed in them often, demanding perfection. Everywhere around her there were shiny orderly antiques blemished with other people's histories, and better yet, some replicas of antiquities which were artificially distressed. All of her daughters were alien and demanding so she went to work at her husband's business and called us on the telephone. She was as distant as a photographed angel—blonde hair and bright red lips. We longed for her. She believed in money and insisted we were poor, but she is rich now. Her money is given to her daughters in lumps as intricate as lodestones. She is still usually farther away than a filmstar. Whenever she visits her daughters, heaven is in the room disapproving. When she came to see my new house, she did not love me anymore. She insisted she loved me once, until I reminded her of something.

I told her I had cleaned, but she wouldn't believe me. For an hour she stood in the foyer afraid to sit down for fear of staining her raw silk slacks on my upholstery. I told her, "Momma, please sit down, have some crackers."

"All right," she said finally, looking at her watch. I could tell she was afraid. She couldn't be sure if the spots on the white curtains were stains, wads of dust, or ghosty floaters in her vitreous humor.

My boyfriend came downstairs and complained to me of a cough. In the kitchen, I took pieces of ice out of the freezer and threw them on the floor to break them. He sat down across from her on the couch waiting for her to address him. She did not. She curled her lips inward.

"She's the princess with the pea. Don't kill yourself trying to please her." He held my wrist for a second while I was pouring her rum. He went back upstairs abruptly to piss.

"Come see the rest of the house, Momma."

"I'm tired," she told me. Suddenly, I felt an overwhelming sadness for her having to survive dinginess and being weary in my chair. She wished I were thin and rich. She wished she were off the coast of Majorca in a boat. She loved to travel and to dress well and to be admired by strangers. She closed her knees. I gave her the drink and she hummed. She thought: "This is like the awful lower middle miserable house my grandfather had in Brooklyn. He'd come over on the boat and he never took regular baths, only for funerals and Easter. When he died his wife moved into the basement and sat by the furnace wearing black. She *liked* the cellar."

Momma hates cellars. She moved to the South because the

houses haven't any. Now, Momma was visibly more uncomfortable. Grey forms were floating in front of her eyes. Trouble with her retinas. She wanted to eat or to leave, but she was sure the kitchen was contaminated. She called to me, "Is there a Chinese place nearby? Do you have any dishes for food?"

I told her I'd send my boyfriend for something and egg rolls. When he left we were finally alone. I wanted her to see how I'd cleaned the basement, but she refused to go downstairs. She asked several times, "Is it underground?" I told her no. She wouldn't believe me. I paused, and continued in a minute.

"Do you like anything about the house?"

She waited, picking at her white silked knee with a sharp hard fingernail. She sat with her knees slightly apart and a tall sweating glass in her other hand. I could see the place as she saw it. Grime on the upholstery and unswept-up dreck in the corners. Particles smaller than the eye can see which I could suddenly feel between my teeth.

I decided to fight back:

"Dolores. You are a pill, you know that? You are squatting on the edge of the chair and you won't let yourself be comfortable. What are you afraid of? Relax, Mother."

"I said it was nice," she said, insincerely.

"You hate it."

"It's nice." She looked over at the mantel for a few seconds. "Are you going to do anything about the floors?"

"Shut up."

"I will not shut up. I will not. I'm your mother. You shut up. You are a hateful child. Lazy. Unpleasant. GOOD FOR NOTHING. LIKE-YOUR-FATHER." She stopped to take a breath. "I can't say anything to you because you are so touchy. How did you get so touchy? You invited me here." She raised one eyebrow the way she does.

"I wanted you to come and say you loved it."

"I don't love anything anymore. I loved you until you were three. What happened to you? You were such a good baby. I remember you when you were a smudge."

"My life is difficult, Momma. I have a life."

"What do you know?" she half-asked, swallowing the end of her rum. She flattened out her pinky and placed it next to her thumb, creating an infinitesimal space between her two fingertips to illustrate the extent of my knowledge. One sixteenth of an inch. I ran into the kitchen and crawled under the skirt of the tablecloth. A minute later she called in a high melodious screech, "BARBA."

My baby name. Mother was sweet again. She radiated in the chair. "I'm sorry, Momma."

"No you are not. I know you. Show me the cellar. Come on I'm ready." She looked at her wristwatch again. "Dirt floor?" she asked, standing up now.

"No. Poured concrete. Laundry. Everything." I took her by the hand. She moved into the kitchen and waited quietly with a look of sweet anticipation. There was something I must not have understood about her expression. It is that intangible, angelic quality about mothers, I suppose. She had acquiesced. We were going to see the washer. I opened the latch to the door at the top of the cellar stairs and flicked on the light, letting her go in front of me holding the rail. At the bottom of the stairs, she gasped, "What's that?"

She was pointing to grease spots on the cement floor. I said, "Something from the furnace."

"Oh. The walls are white." She was looking upward. I was relieved. "I didn't expect it to be bright down here." Now, moving toward the gleaming appliances. As if by instinct, she opened the lint trap in the dryer and collected a pink and grey wad of fuzz in her delicate hand. "Barbara, I want to tell you—" she started, but she slipped on the furnace grease while she was walking toward me, and she sent one of her tiny mules flying into the air.

"AHHHHHHHH!" she said, much more loudly than I'd ever heard her scream. She was unhurt, but she had a sticky brown stain on the thigh of her white slacks. "Get me Carbona. DRY CLEANING FLUID! SPOT REMOVER! SOMETHING. QUICK!" She was about to cry, I could tell the water was filling her as it would fill a vase. Her agitation caused things in the room to vibrate.

"Mother, it is only a stain. Just a pair of slacks. Don't get so crazy."

"You are stupid. You never know what counts. Go get some spot remover. Go as far as you need to but GO!"

Many people were in the street. I went for the center of the crowd hoping to lose myself but her shouts grew louder there. From the gray hair and the orlon hat of the woman in front of me I could hear distinctly, "YOU ARE A ROTTEN DAUGH-TER."

The screen door of a shingled house around the corner from mine wobbled with the words, "GO TO THE STORE FOR SPOT REMOVER. DON'T TARRY. I CAN'T USE SOAP ON SILK, YOU SILLY." I started to skip.

In the drugstore, there was a loud disquieting whisper floating out of the Muzak speaker. "I BET YOU DON'T KNOW YOU CAN'T USE SOAP ON SILK. YOU DON'T KNOW ANYTHING IMPORTANT." I bought every kind of cleaner they had.

On my way back, I felt light-headed. A giddiness surged over the waves of my thought like an oil spill. Outside the house, I noticed one of the lower windows was emitting an uncanny glow, a phosphorescence. I cracked it and called inward and downward to my mother.

"GOOD DARLING." she said. "Drop down the Carbona and leave me be." Her voice was louder and more perfect than I had remembered it. Quite loud. Children playing in the parking lot half a block away stopped what they were up to in order to listen. When I walked into the house, I noticed that it gleamed, too: it had that happiness clean objects possess. I could see a glow coming through the floor boards as if they were lit from underneath. I rushed to the cellar door and peeked down. She was sitting on the floor by the furnace scrubbing her silk slacks with solvents. She seemed in a trance and did not hear me enter. Suddenly awakened, she blurted,

"Oh, Barba. Stay out."

Mother and the basement were cleaner than I'd ever seen them. Everything was free of debris, as if she'd flushed the place out with her tears. The hot water heater, the old shoes and rags, even the cement floor shone. Mother was considerably larger than she had been when I left. Indeed, the appliances and the storage boxes might have fit into her hands like toys.

The next amazing thing: I lost my ability to walk and to talk. It was delightful how joyous this made me. My pimples were gone and my skin was smooth as soap. I was no longer graceless, or anything describable. I waited interminably at the top of the stairs.

"Poor thing, come to me." She finally boomed. And I did.

I rolled down the stairs toward her. She was larger than the basement could hold, now. The ceiling above us and the one above that became elastic as an interior membrane. Soon the upstairs windows were her two open eyes, looking out.

The Winnebago Mysteries

Every typical family at first represents merely an animal connection, as it were, a single organism. Cast back upon itself, it cannot get beyond itself. From itself, it cannot create a new individual and to try to do so through the education within the family is a kind of intellectual incest.

Franz Kafka

The whole family, in a rolling house, can have a new backyard every night.

from a radio commercial for Winnebago Homes and Rollin' Out Recreational Vehicles, Inc., in Highsville, N.C.

A dirty-white Winnebago Itasca with a bashed-in front left headlight is parked on the Pacific beach just north of Ft. Bragg California. It is surrounded by bright nylon tents and mobile homes, and tall evergreens that brush away the cool fog in the early morning.

Two wrestling men come out. Quickly, one is on his back in the mud with his feet on the stomach of the other, a younger man whose hair is yellow. The man in the mud is over fifty but he has enough strength left over from the Second World War to lift the lighter standing boy off the ground by thrusting him in the belly.

For a moment the blonde boy is balanced on Mr. Stark's feet in the smoky air and shouting, waving his arms and legs. Next, he's thrown against the huge rubber tire of the camper. He's unable to catch his breath.

"Ruthie told me you were a violent mutha—" the boy begins in a second. He's interrupted by a kick in the mouth. It begins to drizzle.

The older man uses a Southern accent. "Who the hell do you think—"

For an instant, he stops Mr. Stark with a quick punch in the upper thigh. Standing, he begins to back toward the door, palming the grimy polyester-coated aluminum siding behind him.

"Jail, Buddy-Roe," Stark shouts.

"Look, Stark. Cool it. Look." He's at the steps. The big gray man is closing in. "I asked you to meet me. Didn't have to tell you. I was being nice. Coulda took the Itasca, told you nothin—" He slams the door on the flattened nose of his attacker who starts to bang it. From inside: "Stark. Didn't come from two thousand miles to give you a chance to kill me. You got it? Came to get my van, bud."

"Why didn't you write, say where you were before? Kidnapped her. Statutory—" Mr. Stark can't finish. He hits his knuckle on a ribbed metal band around the window of the door.

"You think I shoulda married her?"

"Why didn't you?"

"Ruthie? Think she woulda stuck with it? I'm a simple man, Stark. Simple pleasures." Inside his RV, Clack Clark crosses his legs at the knee on his avocado sofabed.

"Get on out here, you sick—"

"No. You mean to kill me. Got enough trouble as it is. She wouldn't of, anyway. I said I asked her. I asked her in Alaska one night the heat was out, had to stay over in a—" He realizes the rest of his sentence will make Stark madder. "Ruthie's a prize I never deserved."

"Don't you get smart." Stark cracks the polyethylene window between them.

"Man, I never said I was smart. I said SIMPLE. Think a smart man would of let her go? We have a common interest as I see it. Your wife and your kid who was my Ruthie. Where'd they go? What happened to them? Don't you think a mystery like that would bring us together? Why are you gonna kill me?"

"Son of a bitch."

"George." He puts his nose through the new gash in the window. "I like you. Really." Clack pushes out the window. "Just to show you, I'm gonna give you everything inside here you want. Here." He gathers a wad of assorted papers, letters, envelopes scribbled with notes and typed onionskin. He pauses before he dumps them. The old man is soaking now. The rain is falling intermittently and not far away the gray Pacific is rolling in slow waves. "Here's your letters. Here's their letters. Dear diaries. Every goddamn thing. You find your women, man. Okay?" Clack lets go of the pile which floats to the wet sandy mud. He moves to the swivel chair on the driver's side and starts his motor.

Around Mr. Stark's sneakered feet the ink and pencil marks are fading from the rain. Black and blue rivulets dribble into the sand. He has read every bit of it anyway. He knows it by heart.

Leaving the engine to idle, Clack opens the door only wide enough to squeeze through a pile of sweaters and tee-shirts, a few fancier women's clothes, a big muskrat coat, and two boxes of Kellogg's cereal. Stark pries the door open further and shoves the pile of belongings back on him. Clack runs out of the R.V. by the door on the opposite side.

Alone now inside the van, Mr. Stark notices for a second that a certain snake skin shoe on the shag rug has the undeniable scent of his estranged wife Gloria's talcum powder. Out the window he watches the boy shrink into the distance at a gallop.

It is a beautiful place where they have been fighting. He likes Clack right now. He begins to open his mouth to yell to him, "I don't mean it. Buy you breakfast. It's her fault." He doesn't know which her he means, his wife or his daughter. He has a horrible discomfort inside this thing, though he knows that both women were recently here. A week ago, one of them may have slept in the bunk suspended above his head. He's hungry, his gut hurts where Clack landed one. He couldn't sleep any last night. Inside this van he can smell and hear them. It is a claustrophobic big baby carriage, a turtle shell, a house with a motor, a home you can take with you. It's too easy. They'll have one soon that feeds you and pipes out your pee like an astronaut capsule—Stark hates it.

He thinks of going out into the sand to gather the pieces of paper and stack them into a pile that has some reason to it. He should read his daughter's diaries again from Miranda, his wife's letters to Ruthie, and the notes from Clack. What places did they like? What places would she go back to? He wonders if he remembered to read the backs of every page and the dates and the postmarks, and the parts scratched out and the parts they didn't write.

He leaves the Winnebago home with a high heeled shoe in his fist, and walks down the beach toward Clack's now-collapsed figure a quarter of a mile down the strand. Stark has to tell him how he, himself, is absolutely at fault. Fathers are responsible for their children, their women.

Finally all by itself, the Winnebago moans, hums, generates power, and maintains the damp stinky mold in the shower stall that is the only life form left to it. Under its front tires fragments of the writing are shaded from the rain... "You have pulled my whole life up by its roots"... "Her fanny was every bit of it..." "...Keep in mind you are quicksand to a man..." "You are loosely attached..."

The soaking papers that do not manage to explain anything, especially the last twelve months or the last twelve hours, or minutes, that do not explain a renegade daughter and wife, or anything else in particular, can be read one more time before they disappear.

Somewhere in the U.S.

April, 1975

Dear Momma:

I have sort of left college. I mean I am living in a Winnebago Home, so I have moved. I am always moving. Unlike my sisters, I won't be able to give you an address. It will be Ruth East, or Ruth West, or Ruth Middle, until this travelling stops. If I have my way that will be never. You see, I won't be able to stop anytime soon because he is driving. Since we don't have to stop to go to the bathroom, I don't know how you will ever find me. I have run away altogether.

As you may have guessed, there is a man who drives. I'm in awful love. He will never marry me and he is totally unacceptable anyway, since he's got roots of rubber tires.

Maybe you don't believe me. I can tell you about the aluminum, the exact spaces between the ribs in the bright metal lining the counter, the frequency of gold flecks in the formica, the mileage, the length and fiber content of the shag carpet, Monsanto, that he had especially installed. You would love this little place. I am sure you could do wonders for it.

But Momma, you have always filled everything up. I mean, there is very little space in here for your dear and delicate items. I know what you have is real, and valid, time-tested, and antique. You won't have to worry about me and whether or not I'll be broken, since the disaster, my Irish mother, is here. I cease to be your daughter. You haven't one at college, you haven't one married to blank, you haven't one in California. For as soon as you know I am there, you can be sure I will be gone. Momma, I'm missing in motion. What will you tell the highway patrol, since I have just cancelled what I've told you. Actually I am living in Arkansas as this letter is postmarked. I love you anyway, like the good fairy, like the Easter Bunny, like you love your own body, your own breath.

Mother, breathe, breathe, Mother.

Always,

your ex-daughter

❀

Kitchen Table
Stark Home, Cybil, Texas
May 2, 1975

Dear Darling Ruth:

The dogwood is blooming. The acres of gardens are filling with butterflies. You must realize I am miserable, winter is everywhere, you have pulled my whole life up by the roots. I am breathing and I am fifty eight. When your father brought me the letter I was re-reading Austen, as is my wont, you know, in the spring. Your letter was an event.

You have made me reconsider. I have gone off my diet.

Burned my thirteen hairpieces.

Broken a few pieces of china, fired one of my decorators.

Your father says I did nothing I could have helped. But he forgets I never could have had you. Now that is something to think about.

Who is this young man you are with? Does he handle you badly? Where did he go to school?

Now you may think; oh, Momma, she has only these silly considerations. Well, she does. I have decided you are to be my sacrifice, dearest. It is really things that matter in the end. Remember that, and also remember that to be a daughter is to have a curse. You will always have a mother.

Your mom

❀

North American Continent

June 4, 1975

Dear Momma:

Do you want me to tell you how we do it?

He begins with the unders of my arms, the outer rims of my ears, the spaces between my toes, the red gum under my upper lip. I watch him make love to me in the rear view mirrors, or in the glassy orbs about his eyes. His eyes are LP's to me.

His name is Clack. He says his real father is Marilyn Monroe. He used to be in a penitentiary for selling dope to grammar school kids, but when he was in prison they sent him into the Sierra Nevadas to watch for fires, so he became a mystic.

(I am leaving out here a part you would leave out, because it is too dirty. It is probably dull to you, since you stop at the neck.)

Momma, I'm in love with everything in trousers that lives in this hemisphere. I can conquer them all, and the Winnebago moves on as I do, men following one another swift as antelopes.

By the way, I think I am pregnant.

Love,

Ruth

your ex-daughter

●

Kitchen Table
Stark Home
Cybil, Texas

June 8, 1975

Darling Ruth:

Let me tell you a thing or two. I am capable of making a few distinctions. I married your father because he had the longest shlong in the Navy.

If you are really pregnant, in the normal sense, you should consider settling down and so forth, as you will not be able to ruin your children while you are on the go. It is a full time job.

People mistakenly think women are afraid of bearing mutants. If I'd had a baby with a head like a basketball, I would not have had to go to the trouble of making you a monster.

I am the world, your mother. You come from a long line of mothers, going back namelessly, endlessly into time. You are the tiny temporary period at the end of our sentence. You started out on a bad night. I remember it. I closed my eyes to avert myself from the awful — — — your father was presenting, and I saw a small patch of green sea, like the linoleum in the kitchen. I felt horrible suddenly. I know who you are all the way back to blank. You can't get away even from the worst in me.

> With condolences
> concerning
> your pregnancy,
>
> ALWAYS,
>
> Mom

❂

> North American Continent
> I don't know the date
> anymore

Dear Momma:

But Momma, one day it is Kansas, the next day it's Vermont. There are four babies at least that whine and swell in my body. I think all my babies will be boys.

We have been everywhere and we are going again.

You may have stopped looking but you will not forget.

Long ago you stopped thinking but you will not stop hoping.

Clack told me today he was slipping me a Mickey Finn. Maybe he will make me lose my mind and be gang-banged, mutilated. I write down my woes everyday, in diaries, letters, I xerox my letters to you when I can, I watch myself cry in the mirror while Clack pulls up to restaurants, opens the curtains, and watches the people inside eating while he pokes fun at them, points, laughs, tells them where they can go. They don't hear him because of the plate glass, but they understand. Sometimes he uses sign language, sometimes he picks his nose and eats it. They try to pretend he isn't there.

But he is. It would take twenty women to come up with enough excuses to keep me loving him, and these twenty women would have to take all day, examine him naked, fuck with him, and interrogate him, and still they would have a hard time persuading me. Mother, his short toes and his fat palms bother me. The big pores in his nose bother me. Shlong or no shlong he bothers me.

And no matter what I tell him, he's convinced I'm going to love him until the end of the earth. Like you want me he thinks I want him.

I am asking you for advice.

Yours ever,

X

❂

Kitchen Table
Stark Home
Cybil, Texas

July 3, 1975

Darling Ruth:

What good is it for me to go about forgiving you and giving you advice when you know that you are already over the hill, belly swelling, blank beginnings begun? Already having swallowed all the schlock, you are going to perpetuate it, and I am no one to be philosophical. Don't you realize men are put on this earth to keep up everything inessential?

A man does the things he does so that, when a woman gets tired of him, she can admire whatever he has produced, be it the rent, a garden, in your father's case a row of sensible figures, or an Easter Card.

Eventually she will fall in love with her baby. And the man's uselessness is reduced to a smidgen. Unnoticeable.

Why do you think women have baby after baby like an oven? For entertainment.

My advice to you is to keep your secrets. It is how we survive. Have your babies and you won't be lonely.

Keep in mind you are quicksand to a man.

He has to find you benign.

Your Mom.

P.S. Ruth, come back
to me.

●

Foothills of the Rockies

July 30, 1975

Dear Momma:

Not twenty minutes ago, I started rubbing my tongue along my gums and I found something. I know your tongue very well. There is that space between your bottom teeth to the left that you shoved into being with your tongue, which is, as I recall, a pink and meaty little thing. I remember the time you had ox tongue in the refrigerator for months. They eat it in France.

Well, here in my mouth (I inherited thinking in my mouth from you), I found a second row of teeth beginning. In the sockets where the wisdoms were pulled, a whole new range is erupting. Not only there, but outside my other teeth, new peaks are poking.

I've had friends, momma, women in college. They talked at me at night. Thin ones came in. After their ice cream binges. They came to talk about their bodies. Thick piano legs, pear shapes, whale tails, peanut breasts, one green eye and one brown. The cellulite evil. All their mothers, it seems, were great beauties. They had their mothers to look forward to. One named Laura had a tiny mouth. Once she confided in me that she had two bicuspids lodged in her temples. A canine tooth buried behind an ear. Bombarding her with x-rays, the exploring dentists found some in her stomach, her fingertips, and one poking from the elbow bone. They hid in all sorts of discreet places in her tissues. The teeth were poised and ready to strike.

I told Clack about my new teeth. "Talk about something else. I've got a weak stomach." So I'm writing to you. I lied to you about him. He was never exactly in jail. But he's a mystic. Maybe once a junkie.

Right now I'm sitting on the stoop of our beige and white panelled Itasca, drinking a Nehi. The A.M. rock is about heaven and you and baby and me. I realize I always trusted I could become a beautiful and vapid woman. But that no longer may be the case. Does a second row of teeth run on your side? Poppa's? If I pull them, will they come back like your little whiskered moles do?

To return to being vapid and beautiful. You always promised me it was an option. You banked on it, didn't you?

An exercise:

For a minute, close your eyes. Count to fifteen, slowly, now to twenty. Imagine my bare feet on a layer of pine needles in a Tennessee forest. The two big toenails are still painted Faberge dark rose. I am licking my lips, which are grapey. Return to the unshaven calves. Now my scabby knees. I'm in those sun shorts I stole from you, the ones you used to wear in the backyard in 1958 with a tube top. Now to my scabby knees. Clack gets rough sometimes. My tummy doesn't poke out yet. The little mark on the left side of it stands out against my tan. All the moles are turning black. A Mexican halter slips off one shoulder. The turquoise necklace from Christmas 1972. Face clear from the sun. Buttocks flat smack on the heating aluminum. My back against the Winnebago door. The skin above the elbows is flabby, that's the first place to go. I recall these upper arms when they were yours, momma — they turned into fistfuls loose as jelly in a baggie. I have wanted to poke a fork into you, momma. But you already know that.

I am the last of the line. The final daughter. The genes rest in me like a volcano.

I agree with you. I'm quicksand to a man. The thing about the fellow in there on the carpet is he's stupid. And he has a dumb respect for my sex. When he makes it with me, I feel as if I'm losing my mind and turning back into a mammal. This must be because he is not middle-class. Mammals, mothers, have tits and fur. I am getting up now to go squat and pee in the woods. The action will be silent. Tiny lizards and caterpillars will appear. I'll find two beetles on the moss. I will kiss the bark of trees. I will hug a thick pine like Goethe used to do, for strength.

Why does it always say women are closer to the earth? I quote from a piece of literature I found in a coffeehouse in Louisiana about the Buddha.

*It is scarcely to be gainsaid that woman is
nearer to the world than man, and sexual
differentiation is one of the things which
are "not so, not so" in Nirvana.*

It says later that Gautama Buddha

*called on men and women alike to root up the
infernal grove, to abandon the sexual nature,
and to put on spiritual manhood . . .*

I am tired of all my dull comely beauty. The nose, I admit it's not from your side, does it in anyway. It's more chockful than vapid, more busy and soulful than open. See my hair: it is torn and knotted and fast past my waist.

It says in the same book:

*Unfathomably deep, like a fish's course in
water, they say, is the character of woman,
robbers with many artifices with whom truth
is hard to find, to whom a lie is like truth
and the truth is a lie . . .*

Keep this in mind. A kind of clue to you.

Clue two:

Vulva is a hole deeper than a termite's nest.

— *African Chant*
Unfathomably,

your ex.

❁

Kitchen Table
Stark Home
Cybil, Texas

Aug. 2, 1975

Darling Ruth:

The zinnias and sunflowers are overwhelming the garden. From your letter I surmise you are thinking. I can't remember if I thought when I was your age. I remember I had my mind on a new pair of red snake pumps. Right now I'm wriggling my toes into the nice topsoil the gardener brought in. In my own way, I'm a primitive. Your father calls me a creature of appetites.

I'm resigned to your addresslessness. But I write you anyway. I'm relishing my lament.

Do you still have the problem with your teeth? Nobody on either side has ever had anything like that. It may be my fault— all those tumblers full of milk I had the maid pour down you. I admit it was a mistake. If you were raised scrawny you wouldn't be over-sexed and ruthless. You are a lousy daughter.

Ruth, I am very tired of you. Don't take it personally. I'm tired of your father too.

He comes over to me while I'm sleeping and throws out the orange peels on the nightstand. I still eat an orange every night. I'm tired of his scent and his insistence, and his big grey chest pumping up and down.

When baby boys are born, they spot at the nipples with a little milk. That fact should be on billboards. Your father should know it. It is already Nirvana. He and I are alike as those two boxwoods by the fountain in the garden. The gardener has to think about it hard before he can tell me which bush is which sex. Boxwoods grow very slowly, you know. The tall ones you've seen on the estates we have visited are a sign of old, even ancient landed money.

It may shock you, but your parents are still quite interested in their lives. Your father thinks I'm mourning you, but I'm pretending.

I've been going into myself. He watches the news, whatever is on, and still clears his throat regularly, still wipes his phlegm on his shoe.

You won't let me forget, I'm a Brooklyn girl. I had too many

Reese cups at an unfortunate period of my life. My adolescence was just as miserable as yours. But we couldn't be so self-indulgent. Most of my life I've been depressed. I've always slept overly, liked to eat in bed. An Endomorph. Addicted to food, history, movies, and mysteries.

I started out as a beautiful little girl in Flatbush. My mother, aflame with ambition, entered me in child beauty contests. She forced me to take ballet and tap-dancing with other Brooklyn children who turned into movie stars and producers. As I grew older, I hid in an envelope of fat. All my famous peers have died from brain tumors and alcoholism. The world is fundamentally unpleasant and void of harmony.

I don't identify with the earth. I'm nowhere near it. We have a huge fence around this house and I've got the maid and the gardener between me and everything else.

But it doesn't solve like a mystery, does it? That I should end up basking in the New Texas. That you should end up God-knows-where, degenerating.

In college I wanted a muskrat coat, red snake pumps and love letters from somebody. I also wanted to weigh 118. I practiced walking with my arms six inches away from my hips and a book on my head. I learned to smile without showing my bad bottom teeth you were so kind to point out. Is any of that so terrible?

Now, I have a huge house and an autumn mink and nowhere to wear it. The whole world is dangerous. It is best set and lacquered.

Your father is the one with the faith. I've remained an unstable pagan. I never take off certain bracelets. I've uncanny luck with plants and strong intuitions. I believe in the Great Power of Worry. Recently my doctor has discovered that my blood pressure is only normal when I'm distraught. It is an Irish trait: Life on the Brink. I've been secretly serene since you disappeared. It fulfills a lasting gnawing. Thank you.

Worry runs in the family. You have run off from it but it will catch up to you. Eventually each object in the room will appear perched to fall. Four-legged chairs will begin to teeter. You'll want to rivet everything to the floor, call up the banks, make sure there is no trouble with the charge accounts. See that the burglar alarm is working, the taffeta curtains are drawn, the gardener is feeling well and is timely with the bulbs, that your new woolens are properly cleaned, the front room as pristine as one in a museum, the watchdog within whistling range, the checkbooks straight, the will re-written, the plants fed, the photographs of the lovely daughters on vacation preserved, the vases out of breaking reach, the History Book Club paid in advance, everything just so, for a fleeting second of uneasy bliss, before your father tells me to hurry up. He is waiting for me in the car. I hate it. I hate everything.

He tells me, "Be in the moment, Gloria." That's his god-awful charismatic advice. If he didn't have me he'd be crying on his knees and witnessing to those eggsalad ladies at his church. "You have to believe in something, Gloria."

I believe in things that are put there and don't move: a sparkling house, great art such as the Parthenon, archeology, nylon floors, solid dentistry, paper money in America, and antiquities whose value always increases. I believe in my married daughters' marriages, coleuses, astas, marigolds, pansies, the above-mentioned mink, taxi-cabs, my hair-do, high cheekbones, my Ava-Gardner alley narrow nose, *Thirty-Nine Steps* with Robert Donat, that some races are smarter than others, and that your father is a little bit too honest.

My life, including you, has been full of bearable afflictions, nervousness for its own sake without giving into collapse, alcohol, or excessive use of Valium. Lately my life has been surrounded by beauty they can't take away from me.

I know, Ruth, and I don't want to think about it.

Your Mother.

I am writing this cause she keeps writing and I'm tired of playing solitaire til dawn, etc.

I was never stupid. I worked a lot of overtime after I got out of the community college. As a trailer mechanic in my hometown. At a place called Rollin' Out Recreational Vehicles. I got so I knew them babies like the inside of my head. And I do know my head, since I've been smoking everyday I can remember since I was fifteen and a few I can't. I used to play a game where you make up a ball bearing inside your brain. You roll it around inside the same way you run a pinball machine, with skill and indirection. When the imaginary ball is lodged over, say, your left eye, you try to notice what kind of thing lives in those parts of the brain. Something comes to mind: A puppy chugging down the street on a particular day when you were in fifth grade. Somebody in your backyard during a baseball game grabbed a clump of grass (you were playing the third base he slid into) and there was a brown winding earthworm hanging there. Then you move on to the region around the back of the ears, for example. You will find this pretty hard if you try it. It takes practice as well as sincere laziness. It's hard because one thing rubs up against another thing, and you wonder why you are thinking it. That kid had a sister with a red bush, for example. What you are after is figuring out where you hide things. This kind of research you can do best when you are stoned. It also works if you are going to sleep, or when somebody knocks half your head numb in a fight it limits the territory.

I'm talking to you right from some place right over my voice box, about six inches inside. I got the whole map of my brain from this practice. I also learned that everything in here takes place in the same place. Highsville, my home. I'm in Vermont this minute, but what am I doing? Sitting on a bleacher with a splinter in my ass, it is plain as day, next to my momma who has on a red Orlon sweater with balls on the elbows. We are watching my daddy umpire a J.V. football game. I start to get down with a new woman, and what do I see? A sign saying ENTERING HIGHSVILLE NC BIRD SANCTUARY. There is some broken glass lying in chips on the ground below. She doesn't come, I never knew a woman who would regularly, and what do I see? A sign behind the first one with gold medallions on navy blue telling you that the Lions, Rotarians, Elks, Mooses, and the Jay Cees stuck it up. No point in leaving, they kept telling me. So I took $14,000 saved from all the overtime and bought me a little used Itasca with beige trim, walnut and paneling inside and shag rugs and marine toilet. Then I inherit from my Grandaddy nobody ever thought would die. And I left Rollin' Out, doing just that, and made up my mind to be leaving from then on. Clack Clark Jr., never to be heard of again, exits in style for the rest of his days.

I don't get stoned anymore. I drive mostly. I look at the houses lit up early. I see people eating breakfast, women biting their lips in filling stations while they are talking on the phone. I suppose these people have not been practicing like I have, but if they did I'm sure they would notice the trash they are full of. It is all re-runs going on. For me, it is as if they stopped making new t.v. shows when I was 10 and I took up playing them over and over. That was the year I realized I was slipping. I watched a whole Lucy show before I was sure I'd seen it before. It shamed me. It's the one where she bakes a loaf of bread using two pounds of yeast. Just as she gets back from messing with little Ricky, the bread has swelled so big that it's pressing on the folding dutch doors she had over her kitchen counter facing the living room. Ethel shows up and they start beating back the wad of bread, and carrying on. I could tell you fifty other Lucy shows, and more, that's hanging around from my first ten years of life. My point being you have your limits. Now, near my thirties, the days bleep by so I hardly notice. This is a phenomenon: the slow unwinding. Minutes get more and more alike. They tut over to you and fall into place. It gets to be like fighting your way out of quicksand, to notice if anything is worth recognizing after a while. So I wanted to see something new.

Now, last spring, I picked up a girl hitching in the Berkshire Mountains, which aren't much. But Ruthie was worth my while. She has been talking to me ever since. We talk til both our throats are sore, and then we go to sleep, or turn into a diner to drink coffee and keep talking. I don't like leaving the Winnebago, though. I prefer to drive and yap or do nothing, and keep looking out.

Now, I told her my whole life. But when she reaches up to scratch her face one night, I recall something I didn't remember before: a man who came by in a Hawaiian shirt to ask if he could do the lawn when I was seven. Some crushed hard-boiled eggs in the carpet in my sister's friend Carrie's house. Carrie's momma was the original old woman in the shoe, nine children, and then I tell her about the drawings in that book, OLD WOMAN IN THE SHOE, which I lost from the Emmett Grant Highsville Public Library. And the jerk I went to school with, Emmett Grant the Fourth, and so on. She will listen to anything, and come back with more of the same. The junk we are full of's amazing.

She went to college, and was running away when she found me. But we have the same general tilt. She expects more than me. She imagines that her parents are going to forgive her for getting off their backs, or that I am going to marry her or get her pregnant or that one day the Itasca is gonna be parked. No way. I tell her it's my philosophy not to expect. When you do have all these places prepared life leaves your brain completely and settles into your limbs, where it atrophies. The brain has all the electricity, you gotta see. We see people paralyzed everywhere we go. Their hands are hanging off their arms with no life. They are left at the diner counter facing the pies, waiting.

Tell me something I haven't heard already.

And she does it everytime—how her daddy licked her, how her momma is full up to here with one thing and another. What she keeps from me, she writes to her folks. She also keeps a diary in the microwave, that we never use because it makes food that burns your tongue. Her folks aren't answering because they don't have an address. And they aren't catching up although they may be trying. Ruth tells me they are. She's nineteen, legal. Thinking of her folks after us gives me a little cramp in the middle of my back that I first got when I took a dare and walked with my hands across a railroad trestle when I was six. But it is fun all-in-all. I don't think her parents are going anywhere. There is too much trouble between them, the way I hear it. I think there is little or no hope they'll step out in our direction.

Ruthie is not to be absolutely trusted. She has ideas she knows nothing of. An unconscious. I don't know how or what she thinks, for all her talking. She looks a little like the girl who talked her boyfriend to death in a movie I remember where the boy had leukemia and there was a lot of driving in the pouring rain. And she has long hair she is very happy with. I get it in my mouth when we sleep.

U.S. Interstate Highway System

October 22, 1975

Dear Poppa:

No doubt Momma told you I'm gone. I couldn't even say what state this letter will be postmarked in, as I'm likely to be crossing another one as I write. State line, I mean. All the other lines have already been crossed.

Not to get perseonal, we never were, but what have you been doing lately? Momma may write but I don't get the letters and since you were always the way the world really is, I suppose I can tell you the truth. All I can remember about you by now is that when you sneezed in the car there was an odor of wax afterwards.

The world is other ways as well. We have snow tires and plenty of heat. Ventilation. Reserves of gas and water, a little fiberglass shower tub.

I heard somewhere there is a man who chooses not to wander in his youth. He wants to travel to the temple in the East; but he settles down instead with a wife and family. He is doomed in his age to be abandoned by his sons who go off for the temple in the East. It is true that I'm a daughter moving Northwest. If there is anything you wanted to run away to I will find it. We stop for the damnedest things: stellar jays, sewage dumps, hot showers, stinging nettles. But my seeking isn't the same. You didn't get a son in three good tries. What could you do with daughters after all? We had times of the month you insisted we be prompt about. We had only running hose for church. Why didn't you escape?

I remember the Rudy Geinrich-designed topless dresses in 1963 and I dreamed I wore one to the Methodist Church following behind you, holding your beefy hand, one Sunday. Here is the church. Here is the steeple. We were always the wrong people, Poppa. Un-Methodist, somehow. We wore makeup too soon. Our hems weren't straight, our hair in knots. Besides everything, those pockets of flesh puffing at the armhole seams. Cheap dresses sewn from cotton with bonded foam backing. Big feet. Dirty ankle socks. Something wrong with those girls, people thought. Our elbows were grimy as pencil erasers.

I do not know what you thought. It was the desire that we be beautiful that ruined our appearance, crept into it like the *Edge of Night* across the screen at four-thirty. Four against one after all. Gloria and the Stark girls vs. the character with the wax sneezes and the bad temper.

No, it isn't Alaska. Anchorage was spectacular but when I was there I said to Clack in the bar: Four people in here right now have less than ten fingers. This is a dangerous place, I told him.

You know what he told me? That when he was nineteen he began to hate his left thumb. He chewed away the nail. He let it infect. He sawed at it with a toothed knife. Finally he went to a surgeon. Take it off, he told him. Saw it off and give me just nine. The doctor wouldn't do it.

Clack I'm travelling with is so unlike you it would take experts to declare you the same race. There is more. I'm not kidnapped. This is all willful. I was on my way to Pittsfield or Lennox to work in a little inn. Any one. I was running away. Route 9. This Winnebago Itasca pulls up. All I've got to lose is the people I'll never please, I thought, so in I went. I made up the babies and the teeth trouble to give Momma something to worry about. She loves it, you know. She salivates at the sight of worry coming down the road in a green Chevrolet or whatever. She lives on it like you live on work. The pleasure you both get is outrageous.

In my dreams, I am still moving North. I dream I am in a bus in Greenland waiting for a plane over the pole. I imagine I am in Canada flagging down glaciers, riding caribou.

And we do keep moving. The RV life agrees with me. I do not work, neither do I worry. I write you letters you must savor in my stead, full of everything I ever meant. What do you think? Why do I end up thinking I'm ugly as an Edsel? As deserving as a fat white slug?

Clack says: "You went out on 'em hon. At their house the backyard is always the same one. When I got out of the Army I stayed with my Momma. Day in and day out the aluminum fence out the back. Fucking yellowbell bush. Same squirrel."

Love from your last daughter,

Ruth.

❂

From the desk of
George Stark
2201 High Falls Court
Cybil, Texas

November 2, 1975

Ruth:

You girls were always as beautiful to me as goddesses. And so was your mother until the business with her hips. It was a sign, somehow. Things go to ruin. They get out of control. Her hips, at first, were hidden underneath the full things women used to wear. In the sixties, I remember, when Kennedy was alive, she started wearing straight skirts that rode up toward the waist. About that time your oldest sister had an affair with a choir conducting queer. And we had the house ruffled-up by the other queer, Ronald the interior decorator. She spent all day every day for two weeks sitting on one foot in the living room. Me shelling out. Her one shoe was off: a pump turned over on the floor. The other foot was hiding under her spreading buttock.

Now, I was never a man for boy-hipped women. She was a beautiful low-slung blonde when I met her. But her hips. Women should be careful how big they grow them. She went into the hospital that December but they were still spreading when she got out. Then the foundations came along. So she felt like a horse-hair stuffed chair. The living room was chintz, three times the material any sane people would have. I bought the same things I always buy for Christmas: blankets and spreads; but the faggot had puffy quilty bedcovers made. Pillows everywhere. She carried a few more with each thigh, just in case discomfort slipped in under the door like a thief.

In the late sixties, she's round as a bicycle wheel. Not to say it wasn't old and satisfying like an aged cheese. But I have to live in this town. She lives inside them. They were ever-present, apparent as an un-mowed lawn. Or a state you don't think of that reaches out and grabs you from the map. Iowa. Arkansas. Lydia your older sister finds herself a man with no prospects. And the other one, Gladiola, is running all over Europe, calling home and crying at $7.50 a minute. No fiscal responsibility. Her hips were evident as white horses in the bed. Then the house burned down.

Moreover, we went to visit her in France. Her boyfriend wasn't white. Moroccan, she claimed. And your Mother wore shiny slacks so that the Latins were drawn to her. I couldn't keep all of her hidden. I ordered her to buy English suits cut straight as arrows, but on her haunches, nothing boxy was safe. Gladiola's education wasn't in French, but in cooking couscous. Her fingernails were dirty. The lowlife was showing up on her skin. "All you need is love," she declared. In the Paris Herald Tribune: the riots in the states. Men found your mother in the hotel lobby, her legs crossed, the garter tabs showing. I took her home quietly, in a raincoat. We were delayed twelve hours over Kennedy, moving in ever-widening circles. Her hips were delivered finally, safely, to the straight-back velvet chair that already bore her big depressions. And everywhere in the world there was burning and looting. My two irresponsible daughters were sending reports on worthless types. I found her some new housecoats that winter. She changed in size but never in content.

Meanwhile, you were upstairs. What were you doing? Looking into mirrors, curling your hair with machines. You looked the least like your mother so she liked to call you the plainest.

You went about disowning us from an early age. Did you wonder too? What did she keep in them? The true religion? An account of ancient betrayals?

Now the news is always worse. The best have lost their convention, the worst are full of passionate intensity. The other daughters are married to men I can't talk to. And you are lost.

I believe some persons possessed. She has no faculty for control. She could never help it. I have myself to consider in the end. A businessman doomed to a house-full of women. When I come home, I pick up her panties and stash them into drawers.

Like all prisoners, I have a few moments a day I can steal for myself. These come usually early in the morning, while she is still groggy from dreams I would rather not discuss. The moments are stolen from a life time of bill-paying and subordination. I consider her from a distance and wince at the world. Nowadays I mourn you. Her fanny was every bit of it.

With Love,

Pop

Route 2022

November 2, 1975

Dear Poppa:

I am the one who should take the blame. But I don't put it anywhere now. I don't put anything anywhere.

It could have been your mother after all. The source of all the soreness in this family. She was huge and I never saw her, only the wedding photograph: Your father was the shorter one, dark as a gnome behind a mountain of a woman in a chair. She is wearing a white dress, staring with two shiny eyes at her curious future generations.

Poppa, I think now that the fierceness in you was that little man coming down on the giant he married. You are a genius, as fecund as a field or a forest, who is kept small and angry by those recalcitrant genes standing in the stiff paper collar, behind her.

This occurred to me when I was riding westward and Clack

was talking. Here the trees are already bare. It is September. I think he is going to haul off and hit me for turning on the radio. But men do not hit the women they love. It disappoints me. I sometimes insult men in bars, try to beat them in video games. I want to be slapped onto the floor, kicked, and have the breath knocked out of me, cared for the way I'm used to.

But strangers think I want free drinks or to mess around. Clack comes from a class where it is verboten to slap ladies because it is so common.

I look over and ask myself: Is he strong enough? Is he smart enough? Is he honest, decent, fierce enough? Always the answers are no. I breathe deeply. I tell myself this is my life and there will never be enough.

I am hungry now. Who am I feeding? The mountains I haven't yet grown into?

The face of this Winnebago is broad like yours. It goes 80 if we feel like it. The tank holds 50 gallons. What is good is how the land rolls by, how everything lays down next to everything else.

Clack says we go down the highway to Mexico. I can hardly pee without him at this point, so I suppose I'll go. Sometimes I want to bolt, but then I would have to stay in one place, which is similar to death. This way I am not sitting at a counter, tinking a spoon in a cup, holding my head up with one hand. It seems I've been going forever now. Each day is endless but the months are nothing. I remember owning myself, but only in spurts in bus stations, or while riding Greyhounds and looking at black cities at three in the morning, lit up with pink writing.

It is like this: a crowd of fat creeping days strange as your big white mother, as your wife's still thighs. I am you, poppa. It is my own body I am leaving.

> I love you —
>
> Ruth Stark

Ruthie and me are riding down the road. I tell her I'm hungry as usual. Shoulda took her to Mexico. She's been glum since we hit the flats of Ohio. I don't blame her, though. Cold, purplish. After Christmas.

So in Lorain, in the parking lot of an Amoco station she gets this bright idea we should really go out. Steaks, she says, pushing a wisp of hair over to the other side, cute-like. "Put on your sports jacket." I don't know if she had what she was going to do in her mind all along or not. I said she wasn't exactly to be trusted, but let me tell you the rest.

We get to this "Family Dining" type of place—where you take people after high school graduation. Drinks but no bar. Put me in mind of something. When you walk in the glass door, a bouquet of plastic fruit and flowers sprayed gold for the season is on top of the cigarette machine. Lady in front of us wearing a coat with such a green color it could punch you out, and black fur trim, black hat. I wanted to run when I saw that—sharp and cut out of the walnut paneling behind her like a picture in Sears Roebuck, the kind you know they stick on, the sleeve of a jacket coming out of the picture frame. Lot of people smiling while they were waiting in line, lot of gold teeth. Ruthie looks good, I say "two" to the hostess, we get a little table in sight of the salad bar. "Wine," the whole business, Ruthie says. Okay. But I'll have to get a job if we keep this up. "It wouldn't kill you. Stop somewhere for a little while."

"Why you talking like that, girl," I say. "See all these people raising their pinkies on their coffee cups? That's settling down, simply. You want to try it? They all have life insurance."

The waitress comes by. I say, "Two Filet Mignons," pronouncing the "g" to get on Ruthie's nerves. She has to keep with one idea. I won't have it otherwise. We have to keep travelling until it all runs out and she has to remember that. What else? We sit there. The red wine and the salad plates come. She doesn't correct my "mignon." She puts her finger in the ice water, twirls it around. I have to go take a leak. When I return, she's scribbling on a napkin, and she shoves it under a plate now stacked high with little peppers and marinated beans. Oh boy, her momma again. Little did I know. Relish plate there now, too. Pink table cloths, you know the kind, pile more cloths underneath it. *Oh Come All Ye Faithful* being piped in.

"Give me the keys, honey," she says.

"What for?"

"I've had an accident." I never gave her the keys before. Lock it up tight in parking lots, and keep them on my belt. She's wearing a long denim skirt, and she says she is gonna have her period all over it if I don't do something quick. I would have gone out with her if I didn't have a hunger headache, mouthful of breadsticks, and a fistful of club crackers. I hand them over.

Five minutes pass. I swallow the last cherry tomato of my salad whole. "Is your friend coming back?" The waitress asks, friendly-like. Redhead, natural. Blue eyes, freckly. "Should I take the plate?"

She picked up mine and I tell her, leave the other one. The steaks are served, so sweet. I wonder, of course, where is Ruthie? Doubled over out there on the bunk with cramps? Unlikely. But I finish my steak before I make a move. Can't help myself. Waitress returns.

"Can I take the salad plate now?" Instead of doing anything responsible, I finish Ruthie's salad. She has a hold on me, this is all one big illustration of that fact. I could almost feel her holding down my hands and feet, keeping me inside that restaurant where you could hear cocktailing people laugh in short waves, catching it from one another like the flu. The bottle was half-gone.

"Watch my seat," I tell the waitress with the name "Julie" on a black pin set off by her pink uniform. She smiles. Maybe she was in on it.

Outside, the ice on the parking lot makes it hard for a drinking man to walk. I tread to the back of the place where we put the Itasca. You bet.

No Winnebago.

"Jesus." I go inside. Stunned. Felt like I did in the foyer of Schlather's Funeral Home, a converted Masonic Temple in Highsville two afternoons after a buddy of mine crashed into a tree and was decapitated. Saw the sew job on his neck since they laid him out sloppy. Felt worse than that. I ask for some Bufferin from the cashier. Back at the little table, I think of a thousand ways I knew it was coming. Finally the waitress takes away the opposite place. Underneath, a napkin with a little note written with a felt-tip pen which has bled into the paper. Hard to read. Starts off—-

Darling Clack
What can I say. Want the road to myself. Please
don't send the highway patrol after me. Fate will
carry you along. Don't you know that? You are a
very lucky man. I know you'll do fine. Love you
so much. I'm only borrowing it. Our paths will
cross again. Two dotted white lines. Take care.

— — — — — — — — — — — — — —
— — — — — — — — — — — — — —

Love

Ruth

Well, what do you say to that. The one thing I know about parallel lines is they don't meet. Fella with a mind like mine sits and sorts. Put the woman you love up for grand larceny? I eat her steak and finish the wine. I watch how the fat makes little islands in the cold meat juice. Julie sees I'm losing it.

"My old lady borrowed my RV," I say. Her eyes fold up in the corners. Early thirties, bet she has a kid. Beautiful white skin. "Do you know where I can get a motel room on a credit card?"

She tells me the E-Z motel across the road takes Bankamericard. Lorain, Ohio, in December is not my idea of a vacation, I tell her. She leaves the plates, lets me sit alone with a bottomless cup.

Now two weeks have passed. Julie has an efficiency with her kid Jonah nearby. Picked up a truck mechanic gig down the road. She has nipples big as the tops of two hundred watt light bulbs she won't let me near.

Stark Kitchen Table
Cybil, Texas
January 15, 1976

Dear Ruth:

I read the letters you wrote your father. Recently, we quit speaking to one another, over that letter he wrote you must not have received, since I found it here, the one about my fanny.

We both feel we've lost a leg. We have these oozing wounds. So we keep our distance. He says, as he has always said, that it's me. He says, as he has always said, that I took my daughters from him before they were ever his. I tore you away. So you have no idea how to live as a result. He is the one who knows how to live. I know, he says, how to chew and how to desire, and there are a few things I used to know how to do.

Sooner, or later, I will die. Something, I am sure, will break down. Kidney, liver, glands. He will blame me. Call it a failure of my consciousness. I left myself to be his wife—who is supposed to be in the counting house, meting out the cells, keeping track?

He writes, for example, a note on the fridge:

Wife:
You have botched everything. I am not surprised.
Even you going on a diet won't save us. Eat the
sherbet. Eat it all. Turn the thing over on
yourself.

The Husband

And I write him back:
Blank:
Sooner or later I'll leave you, and I won't let
you back into the garden of Eden anytime soon.
You'll come to my bed, on your knees, I know your
kind. Because you are concerned with appearances,
you try to straighten things out with the wife. A
matter of conscience. It was never love but lust,
later, the Order of the Universe was at stake. That
order is way awry, you may have noticed. We can't
even find our daughter.

The Wife

See what you've done to us? We are wearing out our souls like two opera characters. We haven't the strength. I would thank you if I didn't know all of this already. But I do. I know everything already. It's dull, and he was never as aware as a woman could be. He says I stole his daughters from him. But you were the light of my life when I had a waist, when I still had my moles which the dermatologist removed. They were beauty marks then. Heads turned. You were wearing stretch nylon anklets, and patent leather slippers. Imagine the yellow daylilies in the spring. My white dress with pineapples on the trim. There are photographs of everything. Evidence you had a happy life.

Well, I am going to learn to drive, take a car and go and find you, even though I know this isn't wise. I could be killed. I won't divorce him, merely leave him in limbo where he belongs. He wants to know what he did to deserve this. He married me.

See you soon —

Gloria

❂

She folds the letter and places it in a drawer in the kitchen table. She remembers she is back on her diet and has a banana coming before bed. But she leaves the kitchen and enters an alcove that opens onto a living-room which spans the breadth of the rear of the house.

Gloria Stark is a medium-sized woman wearing a peach nightgown. Her arms and legs are thick, slightly swollen. Her hands are as delicate as leaves. She is alone in the house.

The living-room floorboards are polished pinewood which gleams in the same high-pitched tone as the silver in the glass-faced cupboards and the large chandelier, which is a wheel of bronze swan necks. Through the wide picture window, moths and gnats dance over the flood-lit back lawn.

She walks over to the TV. The late news appears in color: The man speaking wears a white and red window-pane plaid coat. On another channel, across a pink screen with an inset photograph of Johnson County Courthouse are the call letters WACA, behind a bouncing colored glitter which disappears if she cocks her head to the left. She cuts off the set. It pops and turns dirty olive.

There are beige ridges of veins in her puffy feet. Something she read, the phrase "the idiopathic edema of women..." comes to her as she walks on the slick floor back to the kitchen. "...a mystery in medicine."

She makes a banana milkshake with artificial sweetener in the blender. She congratulates herself on losing four pounds last week and her memory slides back to 1946, which was her prime. There is a certain white suit, worn with brown and white spectator pumps—- a W.A.V.E. in Panama, about to meet her husband. She recalls coconut trees and hot winds in the evening. And then she is reminded of Ruth. Her daughter had her fat rump up against the kitchen counter last summer, slurping watermelon and accusing her of something: being a hypochondriac, being menopausal, senile, being unable to retain what she reads. Mrs. Stark was to blame for Ruth's spending two-thirds of her days in bed when she came home. The girl's lower lip juts out above a flat chin. It is stretched tightly over the teeth in an expression Gloria Stark understands as part of a language Ruth invented before she knew what she was doing. It is awful to see one's best features distorted to one's children.

Ruth is ten or eleven, waiting at the table to ask another

question. When she reaches for the ketchup on the lazy susan, she spills a glass of milk on her lap, her father, and the lavender tablecloth.

One of Mrs. Stark's toenails ticks on the dark linoleum as she walks towards the sink to raise her emptied bumpy blue tumbler. Her toes are beginning to curl under and grow misshapen. Soon they will look like her mother's feet did, like bird claws: only bone and skin. Her mother insisted on wearing stylish high heels until the day she died in early February, which was the last time Ruth was home.

The old woman died in the morning. Mrs. Stark held her mother's body as it slowly became inanimate: a sack of broomsticks, then stiffening. After half an hour, she called the nurse.

Now she walks from room to room turning off the lights. With the living room dark, the backyard glows a sharp yellow. Something darts across the lawn. It is a black floater in her own eye: her retinas are going.

Climbing the stairs, she starts another letter in her head. Ruth: You have to understand how lonely I can be. Here with the trees and the TV. Ruth: Hate me. See if I...Ruth, When Grandma died you came home. When you held me outside that unpleasant little church you said you felt the bones in my shoulder, my own arm tight in my dress sleeve.

But I tell your father it's futile. Look at the parents in the newspapers, in the PEOPLE section of TIME. Their children run away. They run after them. Respectable men from New Rochelle have to take time off from their professions to traipse around West Virginia communes and Colorado collectives, seeking out their monster sons and daughters. When they find them, the kids are dying of something and don't want to go. Do we pay for you for the rest of our lives?

I don't believe any of that hoo-doo, but you do arrive with an unalterable set of characteristics, and you keep them. The bits come from all over the family. You come out a tight ball of them. It took me years to unwind you. To find the thighs, my sister's, the nose and the temper your father's, god forbid. The flat chin from Sylvia my great aunt.

Mrs. Stark is in bed, nearly asleep. The women in her family are standing in front of a striped wall. She slides down the bannister into her mother's parlor in Brooklyn. Aunt May's chiffon scarf is dipping into her Manhattan.

She tries to roll over to improve her dream. She can't be exactly asleep, she thinks, but something as strong as hands and feet are holding her down. She can think, she can't move.

A rumbling outside in the white gravel awakens her. Now she hears him in the house. She can tell his mood from the rhythm of his steps. He has been in Houston for two days. He clears his throat at the top of the stairs in the dark.

She sees circles with names of states and other civilizations: Las Vegas, Truckland, lighted writing in the sky. She sees green, yellow, and red wriggling lines, with arrows. She imagines driving right across the map. He is in the room. Forgetting they are angry, he tells her good night, as she follows the small black and red curves to sleep.

After her ounce of cereal in the morning, she makes a list on yellow legal paper.

For The Trip

1. Resolve
2. Driver's license
3. Pair of scissors
4. Mahogany "figa" good luck charm from Rio, depicting a small fist
5. Walking shoes
6. Lime astringent
7. Seven pair nylon socks — one week
8. Hundreds of quarters
9. North American Restaurant & Lodging Guide
10. Little calculator
11. Pearl Tooth polish drops
12. Glue and postcards
13. Nutritious Hormone cream
14. Hollywood carob-covered high protein bars
15. Little book on deep breathing
16. Final plan about my belief and burial in case I die
17. Duplicate copy to the Hub
18. Call to lawyer

19. Cancel Lucretia's shower for January (despise her mother anyway, that toothy smile of hers)
20. Do I tip motel proprietors who carry my bags while offering me rooms? Do I get out of the car to discuss things with mechanics? Do I tip extra because I'm alone? Modern etiquette book.
21. Go to Baker's in Ft. Worth for sturdy shoes
22. Buttermints for the breath
23. Blue jeans (finally)
24. Tolstoy—complete works
25. One of those chinese collar all-weather treated leather coats they showed last spring
26. Lots of paper
27. Coat in cerulean blue, a must. (Is this me?)
28. Some red-snake pumps (!)
29. A fat Mystic powercell flash light, waterproof
30. A card of gas

She stopped and divided her list into three groups marked "Now or Never," "When the Ball is Rolling" and "Along the Way."

She called the local driving school. It would be two months, he said, before she could get lessons. All the kids. She hung up. January now. In two months, March. Then four weeks of classes, and taking the test.

"U-Drive it?" she called again.

"Ma'm. Mrs. Stark. Yeah."

"Would you give me special classes in the evening?"

"Lady, you can't drive, right? How long have you not been driving?"

"Since I was born, I suppose." Gloria lied about her age.

"It don't come natural to ladies your age. At all. Shouldn't drive at night for two weeks."

"How about early in the morning? Six a.m.? I'll pay twice the rate."

"Can't let you do that, lady."

She was not used to pleading with employees. She was beginning to perspire. She thought she was going to hang up as she noticed the dog was scratching at the door.

"Mr. U-Drive?"

"Klimt, Ma'm."

"It's essential that I learn to drive. Immediately. There has been a crisis in my family. Do you understand?"

She heard him talking into the phone.

"Widow ma'm? We have a widow package."

"No. I'll pay twice the rate."

"Uh-huh." A silence. "Okay. I'll work overtime. Charge you time-and-a-half. Six-thirty a.m."

"Thursday. I want to start Thursday. I was born on a Thursday."

"Uh-huh. Give me your address. Thursday's okay."

She hung up, frightened. George would find out. She could tell him her interest in herself was growing, that she wanted to go to shopping malls unattended. She let in the dog and watered the plants. Upstairs in her yellow room, watching the gardener mow, she made three more calls: the public library, the Automobile club, the bookstore for a fresh road atlas and an etiquette book.

Her stomach was growling. She rubbed her left earlobe to stop it, an acupressure technique she saw in Vogue.

The maid came in downstairs. Ten-thirty and Gloria wasn't dressed yet. She called Loretta on the intercom and told her to make poached fish.

At lunch, a limp sprig of something was floating in her bouillon, not exactly like the photo in the cookbook. While she was eating, she thought it was never right to despise your children. But she did hate Ruth now and again. But then, somehow the bitchy letters made even Ruth's nastiness appealing. Mrs. Stark congratulated herself on the hugeness of her mother love which was big as a chest of drawers with a place for everything. She returned to the spirit of the night before. The adventure of the trip. Perhaps she'd been trying it for years, planning exotic two-week trips with George. Jamaica, Rio, Lisbon, Tangiers. Two weeks was the most he would allow. These escapes were always better in anticipation than fact—perhaps because she thought of doing them alone, without her husband. But he was always there in the first class hotel room packing her nylons before they were dry, using the wrong foreign language with the help. She hadn't planned and done anything alone in thirty years, it seemed. Ruth was making her do this. Her life was decent, confined. There were people who admired her. She was aging but that was common. The man on the phone had intimidated her. No more of that.

At dinner George said something about the limas being dry. Why had she put sweetener on the chicken? Why couldn't she give him a straight answer?

Their trouble was over Ruth, but also over his eating too fast, his listening to the t.v. news during dinner. And his mind was full of blandness and averages.

On Wednesday a postcard arrived from her daughter. Gloria didn't feel like reading it. Ruth had pushed her too far already. She stuffed it in her sweater pocket. Ruth wrote these often. Startling, awful things, on the backs of exquisite scenes. She made a point of sending pictures of the Natural Bridge in Virginia with an Albuquerque postmark, so they wouldn't be able to trace her. The letters had been much rarer. Since last April, about ten altogether. There was no way to answer her, of course, but both she and her husband, when they were so bluntly addressed, answered anyway without mailing, out of a kind of spite. She thought Ruth was really irritating this morning.

Spite was everywhere. In the whole family. What had she been coating it with for all these years? There was no more sugar in her life. She wished she could drive away immediately.

She called George at the office. "I'm taking driving lessons. Tired of other people taking me around." He listened, but he had heard it before, and he reminded her he had heard it before. He also reiterated to her all the reasons she had never learned. She hung up on him.

The reason she never learned to drive was her father. He cursed when he drove, and often came home visibly shaken. Forcing himself to relax, he sat in an armchair with a Manhattan and grumbled about Flatbush Avenue. In the car with his family, he stopped abruptly at lights he'd failed to notice, and then Gloria's mother's little brunette head would hit the soft dash. Cars were very soft then, as cozy as slippers. He would back out of the center of an intersection and Negroes in black cars on both sides would honk. From the sidewalk, people told him he was crazy. This invariably happened in the wrong part of Brooklyn—on Atlantic Avenue, Red Hook. Young boys crawled up through the manhole covers to hawk papers or wash the windshield. He drove too cautiously, nervously, slowly, Gloria's father. Even when she was a grown woman, in the nineteen forties, she got sick if she had to sit in the back of the Nash and drive through the city.

On Wednesday she went to the driving school in a taxi to fill out forms. When a plump man asked her why she had never learned before, she told him, "It never occurred to me."

Thursday morning the horror began. She threw up out the window of the Chevrolet all over the letters U-DRIVE-IT. She'd always been carsick, she told the fellow whose Oxford cloth shirt was pulling at the buttons. They had not yet left the driveway. He got out of the car and told her he would see her next week. In the afternoon, she told the maid to fill an old prescription for nausea.

Gloria's father had been a delicate man, half-Irish and half-Welsh, who liked to drink and talk. His silences usually came after kitchen conversations with her mother who had ambition for everyone but herself. Her daughters were to be dancers and beauties, her husband was to be a judge. Her mother, herself, on the other hand, was quite happy to work as a simple clerk in Borough Hall in Brooklyn, to take her lunch everyday and win now and again at Canasta parties.

Rick Klimt, the driving instructor, was one of those persons whose emotions are buried inside young fat, whose thinking takes place somehow without words. He practiced a soothing voice like a radio announcer: *"Take the key in your right hand, yes, that's right. Now put your right foot on the pedal, the gas pedal. This is the gas pedal."* During the second lesson, she backed out of the gravel drive without serious incident. She felt hypnotized, as if she could perform these miracles only at his command. He was dumb and round as the squat little white car they were driving in, but somehow it didn't matter.

Gloria's mother may have known how to drive all along, but Gloria was never conscious of it until her father died. Her mother took the large Chrysler New Yorker out after the funeral on an inappropriately bright and cheerful October afternoon. Two months before, as if he knew he were going to die, her father went and bought a brand new green bomb of a car, the first model with power steering. The new widow illustrated the ease with which she could maneuver the vehicle by turning a corner near the Avenue D theatre using only one thumb. She even giggled, and the giddiness, Gloria didn't yet realize, was a form of early grief. When the woman came to her senses, when she was sure she had buried her husband, she gripped the dark plastic circle with both her hands and rested her chin above it so her nose almost touched the windshield. But in all, her mother did well for a woman apparently expiring from loss: she took up smoking and went down three dress sizes. She grew visibly smaller every day for twenty years. The only reason to live was her grandchildren, she said. Gloria decided that sort of sentiment disappeared in the 1960's. The only reason left to live was a desire not to die, and, more recently, brute curiosity.

When Rick came the next time, things were very unpleasant to her. They went to a place that was formerly a field of oats which was now a mown range of stubble. Rick said he wanted her to get the *"feel of the wheel."* He had a tapedeck "Windmills of My Mind" performed by a thousand strings. She thought that song was extraordinarily sexual, always had. Rick was the first heterosexual man she had seen regularly since she married George, but he was unaccountably dull. In his thirties, he smoked green cigarettes, and talked about his wife who had recent twins.

It was very early in the morning and the sun was exactly on the horizon as it is in this Southern latitude. Gloria never got used to the fact that days always keep the same hours in the deep South, winter and summer. Gloria waited for him, as for a caller, on the front porch while George was in the shower. Rick honked. She climbed in. The sun was so low on the hood that the brilliance confused her.

Rick lit a cigarette and sighed heavily while Gloria bore down hard on the wheel to "feel" it. He asked occasionally, "What's the matter, Mrs. Stark?" because she was not staying on the road, or she had missed a marker he'd stuck in the gravel. She was distracted by the way the world and even the sun moved out of the way at her turning.

"Nothing's wrong." Gloria said under her breath, but she

wanted him to stop heaving and to give up his menthol smoking. The car seemed to be jerking forward.

"Please try to keep your foot steady on the pedal," he told her, and in the same voice doctors use on women, he said, *"Relax."*

The next time he came, she dropped her shoulders and tried to smile the second she climbed into the car. Rick began, *"Today we're going to a residential neighborhood."* She was sure he'd memorized it by heart. *"The speed limit is 30 miles per hour. Let's back out of the drive. Put your arm on the back of the seat, turn all the way around, put your car in..."*

She remembered her skinny mother, at that time ten years a widow, backing out of her garage in Brooklyn. The tension was immense. She screamed at the children playing dodgeball in the alley. The thick parts of her narrow fingers were white around the wheel as she licked her front teeth and started the car motor with the fierceness of a bomber pilot in a Japanese movie.

On the road, Rick continued, *"Keep the car steady, Mrs. Stark... Line up the hood ornament with the heavy white line. Yes, that's very good. That's a good girl..."*

"I'm old enough to be your mother."

"I'm just trying to be friendly, Mrs. Stark." He turned on the Muzak. *"Mrs. Stark, let's calm down. How about it? Is something bothering you?"* In the same voice.

There weren't enough words in the language for everything that was bothering her. They were stopped in the middle of a highway and she couldn't find the warning lights on the steering column. His Kool smoke was filling the car. Her shoes were tight and she'd never driven in heels this height before, so she didn't know how heavily to press the pedal. Her father's crazy comments to every motorist who passed him and her mother's hysterical caution. "Anything can happen," her father told her. "Don't ever drive if you don't have to," his lips folding over the curl of his Manhattan glass, this goon's mouth dangling open.

"Okay, I'll drive until we get to the neighborhood." For once his voice registered something. Annoyance. *"Just, please, take your foot off the brake, roll towards the shoulder, towards me. Turn it towards me."*

In ten minutes she was all right. She laughed. Comforting to have the man driving again. She tried to chat about his twin girls whom he had said were born with "bright red squashed heads." He added, "But they are getting cuter. Lots for Shirley to handle. Cuter everyday. Their heads are nice and round now. Not pointy."

In the suburban neighborhood, she got in on the driver's side. *"Take it nice and easy."* He returned to his monotone. *"Nice and slow. Cucumber. Cool as a cu—cumber."* The muzak again. Blue violins, green smoke, hacking, another sigh. Gloria was dizzy. They were waiting at a stop sign. Above them, a hill lined with scrubby pines. To each side, tan brick ranch homes with peculiar ground level shuttered windows that needed, for the sake of proportion, a good margin between themselves and the lawn. She thought the houses had been pressed into the earth by a powerful angry hand—they were half-buried like faces covered with wool mufflers in the winter. It was a normal suburban morning. Trees, mud, noise of children, the hum of general Thursday business, a potato chip truck, a mocking bird. Inside, she imagined punching Rick in his dull belly.

"Now pull out slowly. Please, Mrs. Stark, may I have your attention, ma'm." He flicked off the music. *"Put on your turn signal."* The hypnosis was not working somehow. *"Make ready to turn right, Mrs. Stark."*

She did not turn right. She went straight up the hill, her foot flooring the gas pedal, towards the newly bulldozed tract of mud which spread out below them.

At the crest, she looked at Rick and saw his motionless tongue. The speedometer said fifty. Faster than she'd ever driven. There was another stop sign at the bottom. She was nearing it at sixty. He yelled. Her grip eased at the wheel, she sat back in the bucket seat. She didn't stop for the sign. A long white Impala hit Rick's side of the car making a huge noise. The intersection spun around them like the label of a phonograph record. Rick drew his knees up toward his head. Gloria was giddy as a bride. Delighted that there was nothing she could do, she let go of the wheel. When the car stopped spinning and the right rear rubber tire went flat against the curb, Rick told her, "You had a wreck."

She sat contrite, folding her hands. He was fine. She was all right. Better than ever. Quite okay. She wished her parents were alive, so she could tell them that.

An hour and a half later, after the suburbanites, the county police, the U-DRIVE-IT people and a quiet argument with an officer, she felt really ready for the road.

"You know what they say—you have to get right back on the horse after he's thrown you," Gloria said.

Rick was idling the car in front of Gloria's house, praying she'd go in quietly. "You are a kinda nervous lady. Probably cost me my job. Get your husband to teach you."

Gloria didn't want to beg. She didn't know how to beg employees. "There's twenty minutes of the lesson left. Let me show you."

Rick ducked out when she lunged for the wheel. He climbed in the other side while Gloria was backing out of the drive. He yelled that the car had to be checked, that it shouldn't be on the highway after a wreck, but she pretended not to hear.

She narrated her own maneuvers in Rick's tone of voice: "*Now, coming to a bend, I take my foot off the pedal and slow down naturally, careful not to brake, turning right in 2000 feet, right turn signal, see? Brake slowly.*" She made the curve neatly. She drove for twenty minutes non-stop, to the U-DRIVE-IT office.

"See, perfect. A Cuuuu-cumber." Gloria said. "Come get me Thursday. We have a contract."

He took the keys out of the ignition and said "Lord" when he slammed the car door. Gloria hailed a taxi at the corner.

In two more weeks, she passed her driving test, first try.

Almost as soon as Gloria got her license, she left the house in a small yellow Toyota she bought cheaply because it was last year's stock. All her supplies were inside, including the red pumps in a new box. The other details were very easy once she'd passed the test, once she'd had the wreck, taken over the wheel, and shoved Rick aside. She actually apologized to him later because she was still a nice lady, but that kind of kindness was going out. She left at 9:30 a.m., telling the maid she was going on a little trip. She left George a note:

Mr. Stark, my husband,
   Kindly notice I've driven off to get our daughter.
Maybe she doesn't love us. Maybe we don't love her but
the suspense has been killing me. Take care of everything.
Don't have a stroke or anything. What did we have a
family for, George, can you think of a good reason? Keep
in touch if you like.

> *Your wife, your*
> *excited,*
>
> *Gloria*

On the road, she planned from day to day, she loved eating alone in restaurants, she read everything, she looked at every person she saw to find out if it might be Ruth. Men would leave her alone.

The day she left, February tenth, it was drizzling, and the sky and the road seemed to blend. The brick buildings, cities she couldn't avoid, and the billboards shuffled past her with a lilt.

Outside Tulsa, Oklahoma, a motel owner told her he couldn't promise heat all night, oil man hadn't made the delivery. He gave her an electric space heater that crackled like a fire, and she had to sleep in her sweater. In the pocket of that cardigan she found a postcard from Ruth, one she'd pocketed without reading in a fit a month before.

                              Redwoods of
                              North America
                                          February 7, 1976
Mom:
   I want you to come find me. Take this letter with you. I will
meet you by a big tree in the spring, by the biggest tree in the
world. I was already there. If you come I will explain everything
to you. But since you won't come I won't tell you where it is.
Vernal equinox, even if that is midnight this year, no matter. I
will be wearing a disguise. Today, I'll bribe the postman to
smudge this postmark so you won't know where. I'm alone
now. I am horrible. You do not deserve to see me. Don't come.
There are a thousand hummingbirds here.
                                          Really,

                                          Ruth

                                 ❀

   Ruth is in one place, after seven hundred miles non-stop, a
short foray in the Sierras, another thousand, and then the Grand
Canyon. Everywhere coldness, wind, hot coffee, blue snow. She
has wrinkles about her mouth now and a face full of

irregularities. On the counter, in front of her, are several Yogo peg board games meant to entertain the customers. The men coming in are farmers and loggermen who talk about sheep and trees.

Outside, the hummingbirds are zooming among the red feeders. Someone like her mother hung the feeders there, but she has not met this person. Every day the large man who runs this place fills them with sugar water. He sells similar feeders at the cash register, as well as Moo Cow Creamers and the peg boards. He wants to avoid boredom in his restaurant. Ruth has been playing Yogo so long that she gets Genius every time now, so that for one or two seconds she feels okay.

Clack Clark
No. 17
Bellview Efficiency Apts.
3228 Labile Road
Lorain, Ohio

February 8, 1976

Starks: Ruthie's got my RV. If you see her let me know. Nothing personal. Address above.

Very Sincerely Yours

C. Clark

Now property is involved. The facts get to George at home.

Ruth has run off now not once but twice. She is driving a stolen recreational vehicle (Winnebago Itasca). She knows her parents still care something about her. She doesn't know where to turn, probably. Wildly, using what instinct she has left, Gloria is hightailing it after her as people do in Westerns.

He is in the den facing shelves of brown and maroon gold-stamped books. A corn on his left baby toe is bothering him. He has been constipated since Gloria drove off. Before him are the scraps of writing from his wife to his daughter, and a list of items Gloria wrote and scratched through, obviously a first draft, that he found in the kitchen garbage. He studies them all, for a clue. The dates to his daughter's letters are erratic. He is looking for a reference to their meeting place. But if Gloria had any sense, (which he has to give her credit for since she had the gumption to leave him) she would have taken that letter with him. The old letters of Gloria's are angry, crazy, not in the spirit she left with. What did Clack do that made Ruth leave him?

He hates certain lines in the letters, Gloria's naming him a "scent and an insistence," references to his "big grey chest pumping up and down." She scorns him and he doesn't want anything more to do with his wife.

But he takes it back. He is actually a religious man. Twenty-five years prove his love. So does the funk he feels in her absence. This peculiar uncomfortableness is attachment. It is the extremity of feeling, the raw end of it.

For half a century now, Mr. Stark has been wanting to fulfill himself. He has thought of deserting his family. He wanders in his job, always choosing to drive and not take trains. He has always loved the road, enjoyed passing cars larger than his own. He takes a perverse delight in truck stops and the kind of anarchy they conjure for him. For a second, in his den, he is reminded of a certain mammoth plaza in New Jersey where there are whores even in the corridors to the men's room: languid, ugly women are swarming everywhere late at night.

At four in the morning in New Jersey before he calls Gloria long distance in the Sun Belt, just as a drizzling rain has started to turn into a sleet that glazes objects, he has had the sense he is capable of anything. The shimmering glassphalt beneath his leather shoe heels could be a table—he is a mechanical toy trudging across it. But he might fall off the table, or fly off, take up an existence in some sense entirely new. These thoughts are dangerous. When they have come, in the past, he has called his wife. He always thinks of Gloria as there, as a kind of condition of his being. As a volcano exists for a village, she exists for him. She is irrevocable, like his citizenship, or his physiognomy. Even in her absence he talks to her. She is in a sense even more apparent than before. He reads one of the letters Gloria has written to Ruth again. "Men are to perpetuate everything inessential." The line bothers him. It is obvious women are at the center of organic life, but they don't know it. Sons and husbands have to tell them. Men are supposed to know women as they might never know themselves, and ultimately, to protect them.

As a way of avoiding the inevitability of their subjectivity, their thingness, women run around half-crazy with minutiae, and thus diminish the world. Flowers, what kind of chops, hair coloring, slippers with a certain dress. Women's minds are made of things like that. It is for men to level and make value, to take over the Great Middle.

George pictures a glowing golden ring, like an incandescent hula hoop. He is holding this above his head while wearing a business suit. It is the halo of the intersection between the important and the idiotic, the rim of being where money, and thought put into action come close together. It is a swarm of glowing workers zooming about the queen, who was always Gloria.

He takes out a North American atlas to plot his daughter's journey. He flips the pages backwards and forwards. He has most of the postmarks on the letters: Alaska, Arkansas, Vermont, Iowa, Florida. He lists the places mentioned. Clack is from North Carolina. He was in the Army. Ruth wouldn't go through Texas. How would they get to Mexico. Sometimes six weeks between letters. It is possible to cross the country in that amount of time. She never says where she is going, only where she might have been. "One day it is Kansas, the next it's Vermont." Not plausible, he decides. Fifty-five miles an hour.

Again Mr. Stark closes his eyes. The glassphalt in New Jersey again. Holding the big circle, he dashes between shimmering points like stars in the tar. He is an astronomer, a wise man.

He puts down his hula hoop. He decides to understand his wife. She suffers from his ability, from his power. His wife and his daughter are on their long way home. He is ground, center. He feels very, very good. He thinks for a second what room in the house is central. It is the bath. He goes inside it. They should be home any day. He is staying put.

The telephone rings.

Stark is washing his hands.

"Hello," he half-expects it to be Gloria or Ruth.

"George Stark, please. Can I speak to him?"

"Speaking."

"Stark, Clack Clark here. Don't hang up. I want to ask you something."

"Where is Ruth?"

"Funny, was going to ask you the same thing. She was thinking of going down that way, to your place in Texas and everything. Seen her?"

"Would I be asking if I knew? Nothing from her. The wife took off looking." Stark sits down on a homey cracking leather chair.

"Sorry to hear that. Real sorry to hear it. Fiberoptics."

"Huh?"

"You know those lights that look like little fountains, rainbow like? Seen 'em? Fiberoptics. Can put little T.V. cameras down your lungs with 'em too. Good investment, I understand."

"What?"

"Don't know, thought I'd change the subject. Damn sad, don't you think, the way they run off. Wife take your car too?"

"She bought her own. A Toyota. Piece of tin."

"Did you get my letter? Ruthie stole the RV."

"Get a lawyer."

"No. Never. She's gonna show up. Don't hang up, George. You gonna hang up?"

"Was she sick or anything?" George straightens his spine.

"No. Got a little thin, maybe. Real nice of you to talk to me like this, George. Appreciate it. You coming through Lorain any time soon? I'm a truck mechanic down here. Richard's Plaza."

"I have heard of it. Highway eighty-five?" George flips through the Atlas on the hassock.

"Drive a lot, do you George? Executive vice-president, aren't you? Tour around to the plants, go see people. Nice life, huh?"

"What do you want?"

"You gonna hang up on me George?"

"Look, Clack."

"Really sorry, but you know, Ruthie was running away when I met her. Route Nine near Williamsburg, Massachusetts, I believe. Lots of truckers go by there. Meat trucks. Anybody might have picked her up. You get what I'm saying."

"You did me a favor? Drove her around for nine months?"

"Well, gave her everything, let her steal my only and most valuable possession. Am not calling no F.B.I., want you to remember that."

"Yes." George puts his finger above the button.

"Should Ruth get hold of you, please let me know. I'll do the same for you. I meant to come down there for a visit, George. You misunderstand me. Really you do."

"I don't."

"Don't hang up on me George."

"If you say that one more time I'm gonna—"

"Let me finish, okay? Ruthie is a good girl and I am sure she is okay. In fact she is real capable of surviving. Something I noticed about her from the first. Kinda fierce, your daughter. You know what I mean? Good-looking too. Tough."

"Done, Clark?"

"Look, I reckon Ruth is gonna abandon the RV when she gets ready. Or maybe she'll turn it in, or come back here to Lorain. One of them. Or go see you."

"You said all that in the letter. You said: 'Ruth's got my RV. Clack Clark.' Is that your real name? An alias?"

"Know how some kids say first Ma Ma, Da Da, something like that? Me, I clucked, you know when you stick your tongue to the top of your mouth and go tuk tuk tuk, like you're ashamed of something? Did that for two years before I talked. They called me Clack. Real name: Charles Riffle Clark. Never tell people that. Hope I'm not boring you, George. Just want to establish contact, you know what I mean. I think your wife and Ruthie'll come back together, we can meet, have a little barbecue, I can come get my RV. I called to say: I'll let you know if you let me know. How about it? Make a deal?"

"How do I get in touch with you?"

"Phone here is—"

George writes it down. "Address?"

Clack gives it and finishes, "Sorry we didn't meet under pleasanter conditions, Mr. Stark. You sound like a real nice guy, a real nice man. Sorry. Like to talk to you about Fiberoptics sometime. Good investment. I'm hanging up now. You hanging up? Well. So long."

George said bye and put down the receiver, and picked up the hula hoop.

Love is a rotten phenomenon, Gloria was thinking. George was probably doing quite well without her. Her Toyota was gathering trash. She'd never thought this would happen—unlike housekeeping, you cannot find someone to clean your car. Fourteen days now on the road. She couldn't go too much longer. Almost March, 1976. A year since Ruth's first letter. They had deteriorated, she could remember. In the beginning, nastiness and silly petitions for pity (teeth, her twice-mentioned fake pregnancy). Then, an indecipherable note about the biggest tree in the world. Somewhere among the redwoods, have to look it up in the Guinness Book. Finally, Gloria could only read the white dotted line in front of her. At times, she hallucinated that the road was a living creature: it is a system of gray blue veins like those on the hand of a dying old woman.

She was outside Lake Tahoe, Nevada, in a hotel with a clean, somehow European dining room. An entire side of the place was a huge picture window facing the mountains which also appeared to her as part of something living, and very tired. Her French grandmother's blue arthritic knee. The woman had doubled over and spent sixteen years in a fetal position in a hospital bed: she could not even move her bowels but she could whine until it almost killed her mother, who told Gloria, *Your French blood makes you precious.*

The table mat displayed scenes to see in Northern California: Coit Tower, Golden Gate Bridge, Monterey, Sausalito,

Chinatown, Wine Country, a drive-thru tree, Fort Ross. Suddenly Gloria decided where she was going. To the only city where mad people lived with dignity, she decided: San Francisco. She knew this fifth-hand. Older women, the peculiar single sisters of her married friends, are swathed in gauze there. They wear flat shoes, have lots of jewelry, and advertise their eccentricities. Or she might shave her head and wear wool suits like Gertrude Stein, drive another sort of car, something antique and kinky. Gloria never thought such things before and she couldn't believe she was thinking these things now, facing Lake Tahoe in a dining room filled with people like herself but still inside their marriages. "It's not George, it is habit." She said this aloud. She asked for her beef very rare because she wanted to taste the juice for once. She heard her dead cautious mother say, "You are going to hell with yourself."

Every place she stopped she imagined Ruth being there. And then she put herself there, and tried to fantasize a life she could lead. If she hadn't George or the life insurance policies, she would have to rely on her body. She realized she might die of some awful disease without Blue Cross to help her. Independence is costly in this country but easy to come by. She wanted to write him a simple letter, *George: You don't owe me anything because my life with you was nothing.* How could she have taken Jane Austen so seriously all these years? She had always imagined that if one had wit, money, or the wit to marry money, life was over, only fruitfulness followed. But instead, it has been mourning, moaning, babies, no sleep, later maids and boredom. Gloria took a very deep breath, and called the waitress.

How I Came To Be In Miranda California, by Ruth Stark the Winnebago Thief.

Dear Diary:

I took the Itasca from the Lorain parking lot in late December in order to find out what I was doing. I used Clack's money from a hiding place under the driver's seat he didn't know I knew about. I had the humming treasure to myself. It has been rotten.

When somebody told me it was almost spring in February in California I went there and got used to the rain. I decided to stop in Redwood country because it is unlike the rest of the earth. I was here with Clack last summer but I didn't notice then that human beings are very small here, about the size of rats. End of January. Green and lush. Inhabited by retired marijuana dealers, ecstatics, and loggermen. The trees persuaded me. I stopped at the BURL COUNTRY CAMPING GROUND AND TRAILER HOOK-UP. I hooked up. Next to the front office were a collection of sliced redwood tumors called burls used for tables in ugly living rooms. They reminded me of tissue slides. All proportion is lost here. Diminishment is epidemic.

There are no blocks in Miranda, only a highway down the center which is known as the Avenue of the Giants, meaning the trees. Off to the sides are roads marked private, mud roads that are colloidal rivers in this part of the winter. On the main street, my place of employ, The Hummingbird Diner, a post office with a master who'll do what I ask, a hardware-everything-else store, three arrows to camping grounds, and signs for attractions like the ONE-LOG HOUSE and the DRIVE-THRU TREE.

February 21.
Today I went to the general store and tried to buy what I need. Burt lets me eat two meals at the Hummingbird, so food's not necessary. Otherwise, a few postcards, some embroidery thread for my jeans, some soap. If I don't start washing I suppose I'll be fired—bad odor. But I don't particularly want to wash or brush my teeth or eat or work or anything else. Somebody is taking my energy and hiding it from me. This is a beautiful, muddy place, hidden by veils of fog and covered with large, beefy men. All I've left of my personality is a sheep-like docility. Two of the herders were in here and talking about dogs gnawing sheep yesterday morning. This passes for conversation.

Sheep are so passive, they just sit there until it hurts, and when it does, well, they bleed and bleat. One of the sheep they brought up had its nose chewed through: just two holes left and a thigh chewed down to the bone. The dogs do it for amusement.

The other herder said he'd cured his dog of the habit. He put him in a pen with a ewe and a newborn last spring. The mother sheep broke the dog's rib smashing him against the side of the pen. At this these guys roar with laughter. Ha Ha Ha. Bleeding from the mouth, his sweet tongue lolling. Cured forever of sheep chomping. No more half-dead noseless sheep. Ha Ha Ha.

While I grease the griddle. I am waitress. Docile and white as a new ewe you bet.

February 22.
It is still winter, but that means hardly anything here except that everything is green, and a few confused flowers from Europe try to maintain their ritual of blooming according to the seasons. The yellowbells are doing it now. Crocuses, tulips, it doesn't matter if it isn't on the calendar. After work at three I hitched into Fort Bragg and looked in the stores. Huge lumber plant there, Georgia Pacific, horrible smell. Plank buildings like those in the movie North To Alaska, put up fast. Gold-rush type wood sidewalks. At the health food store I talked to a lady who sells herbs. I told her about my condition, my inertia, I mean.

She said get some golden seal root and then she said buy some ginseng just in case. She is into iridology. Her name is Miriam.

She looked into the green middle of my eyes.

"You are very loosely attached," she told me. "You have weak kidneys and intestines. Your whites show. Too much pressure on your third eye. Watch out. Try to take a leading role in your dreams. I imagine your dreams are very active now." She asked me, told me.

"Uh-huh." It was true.

"Hold onto your thighs when you go to sleep," she said. "You have too active an astral plane existence right now. You've no energy for everyday, for the material world. Exhaust yourself before you go to sleep so that your astral body stays right where it is. Your dreams are far too busy these days. Give your spirit a chance to replenish your material self."

"How do I wear myself out?"

"Don't daydream. Spend time with living things. If not people or animals, try the redwoods or the ferns. Listen. Do something with every waking minute. You are in a dangerous state—" Her eyes were rimmed with black like Hindu women. She looked for a minute. "Do you know what your astral plane scenario is? Do you remember it when you are awake?"

I told her no.

"No matter. It is usually something you are working out that would only be poorly translated anyway. I mean, you've heard Babcock speak, haven't you? Sometimes it's just babbly stuff, cosmic babble, because there is no English translation for his signals. Sanskrit, maybe." She looked like she was in terrible pain. "Whatever you are going through, and I think it's quite intense on the astral level, well, take it easy. If you should be falling asleep and you notice you are leaving your body, I mean. Breathe deeply, breathe deep gut breaths, touch something living. Do you sleep with anybody? Contact like that will cure you. Get a cat. They hold a lot of psychic energy. You have to clear some space in the intersection of the planes, otherwise, well, I don't know."

"What might happen to me?"

"Don't ever let yourself be hypnotized. Watch out." She grabbed my hands and said something about my "guides." "I sympathize with your plight. It's past life, and spirit life phenomena. There is something tragic there. Stay close to living things. We have the trees here. It is a huge cathedral, the Redwood forest. Left over from Miocene times, from the times when beings were big mist clouds. It may be the forest that is affecting you. This region is an interstitial one, an intersection, an old world. Walk in the forest."

I suppose I should have been frightened instead of thrilled. She went over to measure out camomile for somebody. I listened to see if she said the same thing to him. She wore a Chinese print apricot dressing gown opened like a robe over blue jeans and fancy striped socks, flat foot-molded sandals of cowhide. Behind her on the bulletin board were posters for curing baldness, the Astrology seminars at the College of the Redwoods, and one announcing that this person Babcock was giving a reading, that is, a spirit reading—he's a medium.

There was a photograph of his face in a disgusting grimace—his eyes were rolled towards the back of his head. Trance. She flashed me a look from over by the cash register. I was scared of her. Her orange robe billowing out behind her, she neared me again. She had thin legs and a big stomach, hair clamped back and cracking around the barrette. "Oh. I saw your aura for a minute," she whispered. "From a distance. Excuse me. I couldn't help myself. I'm prying." She took something from a plastic display on the counter. "Take this. Rub it on your forehead. It concentrates healing energy. The spirit plane can be a dangerous place. You have a body, keep it up. Cleanse it. Good-bye."

I left without paying. She'd given me something called Tiger's Balm, which concentrates, etcetera. Chinese petroleum jelly with a little mentholatum.

February 23.
Canna lilies now, mid-winter. Not the real earth. Some place else, left to us from Miocene times.

I am beginning to see what she meant. At night, this sensation of not being able to move my limbs, stuck in the bed, fierce, snorting fright, but no results. Can't get out of bed, can't move towards the driver's seat in this shag tomb. Stuck. No sleep.

I get up. I go to the armchair, and I swivel it around to where I used to sit and look out, like Clack wanted me to.

I move over to the wheel. I think of starting it up, but I can't. It is attached by wires and its big tires are stuck in the mud. Stuck.

But I am still really in the fold-out bed. There she is snoozing, flat out, her hands outside the covers as she was taught to sleep. A big curling wave forces its way over me. It is made of nacreous particles, gleaming. I am sifting away like a dissolving sprite. Yes I am. The interior here moves in waves, too, the carpet undulates. Deep gut breaths, I remember she told me. Big gut breaths. Yes I am. Stuck. She that dissolves slips through the Winnebago window cracks, me, helpless and wooden. Into the forest.

Next door in a truck camper live a retiree and his wife. Their lights don't go on in the commotion, but outside her window, I see the floating head of an alligator which is bothering her dream. I can understand it. He is dreaming of the Everglades and of a certain marina...Suddenly I know everything.

Starlight Hotel
Suites and Kitchenettes

"In the Heart of the City Where You'll Leave Your Heart"
March 2, 1976

Ruthie, Ruthie!

Your mother is in San Francisco. How about that.

I live in a residential hotel for transients. This city is like heaven to me. I feel that I've died and already gone there, heaven, I mean. I am in a state of suspenseful resurrection. End of the world, this place.

There is a very old lady across the hall who has tatoos on her shoulders. She sings at night, and her skin is like oiled wood. Oh there are so many places to shop. But I don't see the point any more, to shopping, I mean. She told me the other day that I seemed like a woman who has lived a whole cycle and is ready to go around again. I am. It rains every day here. I do look for you. I thought I saw you the other day on Polk Street when I was there buying roach powder. I saw a young girl in jeans and that same red Villager sweater I gave you in Christmas, 1970. She had on flats, and her hair was as tangled as I remember yours. But she disappeared as I chased her. Others seem to float upward into the drizzle, the air whistles through their ears. My brains gobble this air. It is as if I no longer have to eat. I need less water. There is a leathery man who swims in the Bay I watch every morning I get down there. He must be seventy. But no, he is really one-hundred-and-seventy. He carries on this ritual as others keep up their little habits in the tomb. They grow nails and hair. He continues to swim, though dead, in the freezing Pacific. One is so energetic on this coast!

I told the woman across the hall how old I am. She said, "Seven times eight, it adds crosswise to eleven. A mystical number." Hoodoo is okay out here. I listen. How can this be the real world? No seasons, no grime.

I want to leave. I have a Toyota. I haven't told you before. But I drive. I make do. I sold what I brought with me, which includes my mink, my French boots, some reasonable diamonds, some Halston leather luggage. Two thousand dollars. I don't know yet how I feel about being this poor. It is temporary, I know. I'm drifting towards you and when I find you we will figure out how to make a living. A recycling shop, perhaps?

A woman my age shouldn't be doing these things. I ought to be sitting by my husband in Texas exploring our love, I know. What did we do with it? Doled it out in little parcels for products: the houses, the cars, the daughters. I still hear in my brain this bizarre idea that you belong to us, that you owe us something. I've had flights riding up these hills in buses. I've thought: I had a child. I named her Ruth. I had her because I didn't have much else to do which was acceptable in Central Texas. Also we were ready for a boy. Girl, though. Husband was a little angry. She was all right, but she started going sour shortly. Whiney attacks. Histrionics. Telling the truth. Nasty. Plain nasty. Why did I have you? What business did I have having you? How could you be any different from me? I hated you for a good while last summer. Now, only now, do I long for you. I am becoming you. I've run off. How about that? Top of the hill, I get off and change.

The woman across the hall has a mantel full of books from Hong Kong she buys in Chinatown. She claims to understand huge textbooks in characters with line drawings. Lion this and tiger that. When you ask her name she tells you, "They call me Leda."

Ruth, I'm coming toward you, I know it. Leda sent me to some second hand shops to sell my clothes. I did. But on my way out of a place called Reprise, I saw a woman like myself. My former self: well-dressed, idle, and made of sharp points. High-heels, long red fingernails, spikey jewelry, razor dogteeth, glistening hose, extraordinarily accurate eyeliner. She was holding a heavy muskrat coat she said her dead aunt had left her. She held it with her arm outstretched, as if she were going to catch something from it. It was beautiful. Worn but gleaming. Because I knew she didn't want to go into a place like that one, I gave her fifty dollars right on the sidewalk. Muskrat is outrageously out of style. "Just glazed," she told me. "Belonged to my mother first. In the family. Funeral just over. I've so much to do."

She could have been me. She has nothing to do but represent herself. I know. She was me. But she wouldn't walk up the street next to me because I belong to another class now. What do you think of that? *De trop.* Your mother.

Leda told me to go north. So I will. You are in the redwoods somewhere. I have your note. I'll read this to you when I get there. I'll give you the fur coat for a peace offering.

Oh I am breathing.

                                                                Love, Mother

❀

March 10.
More of the same. Such inertia that it is impossible to rise out of bed with my whole body. And then there is the lady in the rearview mirror. I look at her for company. I hear the rattles of the old couple next door, and I hear the whoosh of the way-up trees sleeping and awake. I only know Miriam whose remarks do not make me any happier, just sadder to know that I have to spend so much time bandying about above my own head. When will this be over?

March 14.

Dreamed Momma was here in a chiffon nightgown, pale yellow, a very vivid palpable dream. She said she'd be friendly. She helped me clean the place. Then she said, "How many miles to Palm Springs?"

Left the camper quarter to two, intact. Nobody and no sound except the logging trucks on the main highway. Went out to it, and gathered chips of redwood bark that fly off the trucks which are big as houses, and chained on the flat beds. Walked across the road and out of Miranda along the Avenue of the Giants. Could walk it in my sleep at this point. Looked tough, kept hands in pockets. Roadsides are safe. I look like a man anyway, in Clack's orange neon jacket. I hope he is warm where he is. Went to a tree and sat next to it, hugging for ten minutes. Began to cry.

Slept until sunrise which comes early. It is almost spring. Out of my mind with the sharp early sun and the ferns huger than me, and the soft woods. Went to work from there. Ecstatic for five hours.

March 1.

If I count all the days I will not be as sad. Perhaps when the rain stops and the place dries and turns golden, as they promise it will, I can go off again. Wrote to Momma over a month ago the last time. Have to start writing to myself. She probably burns the letters anyway. If she were coming after me I would have to keep running.

At the Hummingbird. Push those MooCow Creamers. Yogo peg boards.

They chain themselves to the trees here, the ecologists. I am never hungry. They don't want any more cut away. The forest is very thin as it is, the forest has its own weather like certain people. Have pimples, must be the overactive astral life I'm leading. Nothing down here on this plane. Boss keeps those birds whirling from feeder to feeder, they're visible only if they are standing still.

March 5.

Spent the night not sleeping.

Stared into the black windowpane glass for two hours, suddenly the face stared back. Not friendly. A smirker. I ran outside. The old couple, I think they are lost, I think they think they are in Pasadena, heard me slam the Winnebago door. Turned on their night light. The rain rattles their overhead plastic tarp. I had to get out of the park. Took a walk, to a stream. But she was following me, the smirking one from the windshield, giving me the shivers. I had to run.

March 20.
I still do not understand anything. All this detritus is washing up before me in my dreams, oozing out of my skin. I am sadder and less than I have ever been. I never knew how little I was. Nobody has ever been less than I am right now. Even my personality has left me — it went to live in the windshield. Her smile, whoever she is, exists for the rear-view mirror. Glad I left Clack. Had to, as I was disappearing. Process continues. Nobody to feed anymore.

Have had the same box of cereal for three weeks. Burt at the Hummingbird gave me extra time for lunch, tried to smile, said he had a picky appetite himself. It took me a minute to guess who he was talking to. I forget to eat and get sick headaches, then I am the steely border in my own brain. I have turned into a speck, a vague idea.

Then there are the walks at night. Three, four, five hours. Deeper and deeper into the forest, to sit under those trees and say, this is it, exactly. Don't know what in the morning.

At lunch today, I waited on a large lady in a muskrat coat. A big, ratty thing. She looked a little crazy: high heels and rolled-down orlon socks, no makeup. Hair tied up in a scarf. Wizened. Peculiar looking.

She kept staring at me. There was a knifiness in it, her look. Can't explain it. Gave me goose flesh. Must have known her in another life.

Gloria walked into the Hummingbird Diner in Miranda, California at 11:06 on March 20, 1976. She saw some rusty brown hair down the back of a girl in a pale green double knit uniform and decided it was her Ruth. When the girl turned around, it wasn't.

She was too thin and her complexion was too splotchy. She had furrows about her mouth in place of fat cheeks. It gave Gloria an awful start to see the wrong girl in her daughter's body, so to speak. She stared at her intently. A wave of perception passed between them and landed right below the point where Gloria's ribs meet. It must have disturbed the girl for she didn't look at her the whole time she served the dinner.

Food was bad: grape jelly in a tin with the white toast. Something called Moo-Cow creamer for the coffee.

She wanted to ask the girl if there was anything she could do for her, but there was no way to tell if she would be receptive. Besides such overtones are not interpreted as mother-love anymore. So she left an enormous tip.

From Miranda, Gloria went north to Ft. Bragg to buy an orange plastic pup tent in a liquor store outside of town. She was going to camp in front of the largest redwood tree in the world and see if Ruthie would show. If not, in two days, she would get the starter fixed on her Toyota—there had been trouble with it since she left San Francisco.

She would know by the beginning of spring, one way or another.

Ruth left work March 21 and went home to nap. She slept straight through to eleven because she was filled with lethargy as if she had taken a potion. Near midnight, she went walking.

As she was hurrying down the Avenue of the Giants on her way to the Rockefeller Forest, she took flight. First, a few high jumps, but later, by 11:50, she was skimming along the surface of the air in a pattern similar to that of certain winged squirrels. She understood this immediately: it was due to her fasting and to her confusion that she flew. She could see her two trousered legs forming a shadow in the shape of a "Y" on the surface of the highway below her. At the hugest tree in the forest, a tree so large it takes a walker one-half hour to hike its circumference, so enormous humans have been known to forget themselves and their purposes in its presence, Ruth landed. She hid in one of the cracks of its bark.

A minute passed. She could hear the hushes of the animals and the whistles of cars half-a-mile away on the highway. The place was still. It seemed to her that space and time were very close together. Whatever she saw shimmered.

She was afraid of the tent and an invader, also afraid of the noise her own feet made since it seemed someone was following her as she walked around to the other side of the trunk to hide. She would sleep there, in another groove of the bark.

Gloria heard footfalls. She took out her large bullet-shaped flashlight and looked for an instant at the brown glow it made in the pine needles outside her tent. Her face and thighs were dented and marked from sleeping on the bark chips beneath the thin nylon floor of her small zippered space. Since she could not stand inside and since she was afraid that if she climbed out rear first her center pole might collapse, she straightened her knees and crawled forward on her hands and fanny, a comic way of walking she had learned in Slimnastics class. She called Ruth.

Who was crouched out of the way of the moonlight. Now she knew she was hallucinating. Never her mother's voice. Never here. Ruth stayed hidden, and imagined swooping upward like a hawk out of danger. It happened. Perched now on the first branch of the tree, perhaps one-hundred fifty feet in the air, she couldn't see the face of the figure in the dark below her. But the shape had a frumpy running gait like her own. She was afraid it was the smirker from the glass. The voice was someone else's, though. She glided downward. When she tried to hover, she dropped, knocking her chin and biting her tongue.

The noise of her fall seemed to cause the other steps to quicken and become louder, then louder still.

When Ruth stood, she knew she wasn't injured. She started to run miles an hour around the redwood trunk. She stopped for a minute to make sure the footfalls weren't her own. Someone was coming. When she decided to take off into the forest she knew she was lost. The ferns were high as her face. She couldn't fly anymore because she was afraid of falling again. Until she lost her breath, she ran. It was unbelievably dark, so dark she could assign any color to any shape and her eyes would agree. The ferns might have been red as well as green, and the floor of the forest could have been blue as well as tannish brown.

A vague yodelling came from her right. It was haunting, as important as something in a dream. She wanted to go near it even though she was sure its source was an enemy. She wanted to pick herself up, but a tugging like an invisible monster was holding her down. She could almost hear the gravity, mixed with the fading sizzles of passing cars, and the noisiness of air moving in a forest, and the calling of her first name louder and then fading. She seemed to sit on the floor of the forest on her haunches for several years, hearing her name being pleaded to.

Gloria yelled all she knew until she was hoarse. She was moving more slowly now and her spiked heels sank into the sod. To keep herself going, she compared the misery she felt with all the other misery in her life. This was the most entire sadness she had ever known, she thought, as she fell to her knees and curled up in a huge round space shaped like her imaginary death.

She sat in a hollowed redwood log which was round and difficult to stand in, like the Barrel of Fun at the entrance to Steeplechase Park in Coney Island that she forever fell down inside of when she was a child with her mother. The Barrel rotated slowly and was meant to amuse people by ruining their balance, but to Gloria it was torture: two heavy men eventually loaded her body, reduced to a lump, out of the barrel and into an amusement park that was packed with more frights at the cost of a ticket. Gloria wrapped herself inside the fur coat, and commenced dreaming.

A little rain fell. Ruth crawled until she couldn't feel the drops on her head anymore. She would burrow until morning. She was very small now, and inside something as smooth as a ceramic cup. Moving toward the bottom, she felt a soft fur like that of a rodent, and a warmth, and she fell in love. She decided to hibernate, and to turn into the mammal next to her. She wanted to learn to think in her spine.

Ruth woke up with a tuft of muskrat fur in her left nostril. She sneezed. Suspended over her thigh was a striped orlon sock with a gleaming red pump at the end of it, a high-heeled shoe. Beyond that was the black smoothness of the inner lining of a burnt-out redwood log on its side. Out the hollow hole behind her she could see waist-high horsehair ferns, and maidenhair ferns, and webworks of poison oak. She realized her head was on the bum of a living being with shoes and socks. It was probably a woman, from the size of the half-manicured hand poking out of the furry pocket. She decided who it was.

"How did you get here?" She hit her mother on the fanny to wake her. She called, impatiently.

The brown mound stirred and sat upright. Ruth was quite happy. Her mother wasn't wearing make-up. She was as messy as herself. There were lines around her eyes.

"You." Gloria said. "Ruth." She reached for her to hug her. She had been dreaming of her husband's face without its body, a talking head with a shining lasso around it, telling her, *You will come around bitch.* She was glad to be awakened. The two of them held on awkwardly for a minute.

They let go. Ruth felt funny touching her. It was as if there were only one surface, one skin—her mother's. Her own was superfluous. Vacant. "Why do you look so strange?"

"Been driving for weeks. On the road. Marvelous, isn't it?"

"You can't drive. Who drove you?"

"I can. Why do you always assume the worst? I left your father. Great news, huh?"

"You left poppa?"

"So what," Gloria said. "Aren't you glad to see me?"

Gloria remembered his middle just above the belt in a bottle green polo shirt the last time she saw him. His huge hands in the cheap gloves she gave him for Christmas.

"Uh-huh." Ruth said.

"Well, don't knock me over with enthusiasm."

"Just woke up, Mother." Ruth felt twelve or thirteen, not nineteen. There was an old feisty invader in her brain. "Let's get up, it's cold. I've got to get to work. Where did you get that coat?"

"You have a job?" Gloria saw the uneven brows Ruth over-plucked when she was ten. Why hadn't she listened about the hair on her body?

"Yes. Work and sleep. I'm very depressed. I don't know what I'm doing here. Do you?" Ruth passed her fingers across her dirty scalp. "Did you get the letter that said I was working?"

"No." Gloria wrapped herself in her fur as she stood inside the hollow. She took an enormous breath and opened the coat to her daughter. "I bought this for you."

"Little ratty-looking, don't you think? You did come into the Hummingbird the other day. You know I didn't recognize you?"

"You wouldn't look at me. You looked terrible."

"So do you. Right now." For three or four more minutes, Ruth didn't say anything else. Her mother's body meant too much. It was horrible to be near it. About three feet away, she said, "I stole the Winnebago. It is parked in town. Work and sleep. That's all I do. I'm so glad you are here." She thought she would cry, but she didn't feel she really knew the lady with her.

"Don't complain." Gloria tucked her daughter under the muskrat and they got out of the enormous tree. She thought she would say something appropriate to her daughter's obvious distress, but she couldn't think of anything. They hobbled like a four-legged creature, a marsupial, perhaps, over to the Japanese car. Ruth was under her mother in the fold of her fur. She almost tripped her twice.

"You undo the tent. I have to see if it will start."

Ruth did what her mother said for a few minutes, without thinking. Gloria asked, "Where did you get that awful jacket?"

"Belonged to Clack, who loved me," Ruth blurted.

"Hard to believe." Gloria waited a second, then she said, "I didn't mean that. Fix the tent. The bag is in the hatchback, here's the key. I've loved motoring. Really fun."

Ruth unplugged the stakes of the tent, thinking all the while that she should be nice. She had to be dear and decent. Amenable, at least. She came from a home she'd broken all by herself. Her plain nothingness she'd been chasing after was an atom bomb. The zero she was had turned fat and juicy suddenly. Her mother needed her. Her mother looked like a wild woman at close range. Hair was threaded with feathers, pins, and pine needles like a jackdaw's nest. Her tweed skirt was rolled over twice at the waist and the lining of the front pockets was sticking out on both sides. Her round flat knees were grimy and stuffed into orange and yellow horizontal striped socks Ruth couldn't get over. Shiny red spike heels, too, circa 1959. "Where did you get those socks, Momma?"

"Something wrong?"

Three times the motor twicked and then died down with a rattle like a loud zipper. "Sparks." Ruth told her. "Come on Momma."

"It is not sparks. Something with the starter. I know this car. What do you know?"

"Come on, Momma, we'll go get the Winnebago, come back, and jump start it or something. I gotta get to work. We can hitch." Ruth led her frumpy mother by the hand, showing her the poison oak along the path.

"Darling, I want us to start a shop in Oregon. Or maybe Mendocino. A second hand shop—clothes, appliances, everything. You get tired of everything new. I still have a little cash. I loved the little places in San Francisco. What do you think? How about Fort Bragg? We could try there. A little store front. Maybe call it "Stark and Daughter" or "Stark and Stark." Something cute, or evocative: "Demeter and Persephone."

"Dumb idea, Momma. We don't know anything about business." Suddenly she felt extremely sorry for her mother. "No.

Maybe we could. Don't you have some flats, Momma. Highway is a half a mile away."

Gloria flopped down and pulled some walking shoes out of her enormous canvas shoulder bag. While she was tying them up, she said, "Ruth, I came all this way. We are going to have a life, don't you think? Aren't you happy I love you? That I left everything for you? You are a thief and I am an estranged wife, I'm sure George has a replacement by now. All our other affections are alienated. We've only our own. Show some enthusiasm or I'll force you to." Then she smiled.

"When'd you get so tough, Momma?" She held her mother by the arm until they were at the highway. At six-fifty, they reached the Itasca. Neither one of them could think of anything important to say.

At the sight of the interior of Ruth's camper, Gloria remarked, "Slovenly. You didn't get so sloppy from my side. It smells in here. Does the toilet work? You said you had one."

"You clean," Ruth answered. "I have to go talk to my boss. I'll quit."

"Couldn't you have paid someone to come in and clean?" Gloria remembered that was a remark from her other life. "Take a few hours a week, even. What is that smell?" She was dizzy from it. "My mother would have said, 'Wreck of the Hesperus.' " Gloria couldn't be kind. It wouldn't come out. Ruth was her embarrassing flesh and blood, the closest one, the last daughter, nineteen years separated from the end of her own youth. Her progeny, standing next to her with pitted cheeks.

"Shut up, Momma. You hear me? You don't have room to talk." She slammed the thin little door and hurried over to the back entrance of the cafe. Gloria sat on the floor and wanted to cry. Returning, Ruth was quiet, almost somnambulant. She walked around inside picking up, piling, making her bunkbed, and tripping over her mother who had not moved from the middle of the floor.

"You don't look pregnant to me," Gloria said to her. "Why did you write such a thing?"

"I thought I was."

"Why did you tell me, 'You stop at the neck.'? What a horrible thing to say. I do not stop at the neck. Never did. I wrote you back. I wrote you every single thing. George has the letters now, I suppose."

Ruth climbed into the driver's seat and started the motor.

"Why won't you stop and answer your mother? Why are you so recalcitrant? What made you that way? You always were, I can't stand it!" Gloria climbed into the seat beside her daughter. "What's wrong? What did I say?"

Out on the Avenue of the Giants, Ruth told her Mother, "I never expected you to come. You came, didn't you? How is it you want me to act? I'll act any way. Any way you say. I'm miserable. I can't remember being otherwise. Can't explain it. Never could. Maybe I came out funny. Part of my mind is damaged, the part that is supposed to be pleased. Is it Poppa? Is it you? I'm a lump. A dodo. Every morning I wake up and have to start from scratch, the whole thing over and over. Is it poppa? Is it you? I ran off and it's the same. Where do you want to go? What is it you want to see? Tell me. I don't know. I don't read your mind. I don't know. I don't know. I really don't."

Gloria said, "There is nothing wrong with you. Don't upset me. I'm fifty-six. I thought we could be together. Nothing wrong with you. You are normal. Perfectly normal. Everybody's children fly off the handle these days. Something in the air. You are normal. I know it."

"How am I supposed to be? I'll do whatever you say. What is it I owe you? Do you look so disappointed because I'm supposed to be perfect? I wish I were dead."

"Shut-up, Ruth. Don't say that. I love you. Stay on the road. I came all this way—"

"I'm grateful. You gave me all this, but I've got no middle. I'm nothing. I will not stay on the road." Ruth felt herself shrinking in front of herself. The machinery of driving was even escaping her. Foot on gas pedal. Left foot on brake. Right foot on gas. Numbers in front. Dotted line. It was too much to think about. Gloria began to rise in her chair. The Itasca was swerving in its lane on the Avenue of the Giants. The scale made it seem like a toy next to the trees which were very serious and the sun blinked on and off through the trunks. Suddenly she lunged for her mother.

"You are the Wreck of the Hesperus. I didn't ask you to come here. I hate you. I want to be dead. I really do."

"No you don't. Yes you did."

"I did not."

"How can you say such a thing? What did I do?"

"You wanted to get some trash in your life, slum a little. Something to do. Get out of here." Ruth reached for her mother's head, pulling a hank of grayish blonde hair.

Gloria stood and slapped her. "What did I do? I'm your mother!"

They went off the road.

There came a very loud bunk.

The Winnebago was crossways in the middle of the highway, its left-front headlight stopped by the trunk of a four or five hundred-year-old sapling redwood. The two women shouted and screamed, scratching at one another's hair and cheeks, until Mrs. Stark took off running toward the grove where her car was waiting.

Ruth ran in the opposite direction, pulling wads of hair out of her own head, and throwing them into the forest, feeling half-wonderful.

Left to itself, the Winnebago moaned, hummed, generated power and maintained the damp mold in the shower that was the only life form left to it. Lights were on inside, its siding needed cleaning. The radio was playing static, and the stained shag carpet, if observed long enough seemed to heave up-and-down as if it were the pelt of a panting mammal.

The state patrol found it and located its owner by noon the following day. The officer told Clack Clark long distance, "You gonna claim her? Shame, you know, spooky, too. Beauty like that, bashed-in, all this junk inside her."

FICTION COLLECTIVE
Books in Print

Order from Flatiron Book Distributors Inc., 175 Fifth Avenue NYC 10010